HOPE STUMBLES

AFTER THE EMP BOOK EIGHT

HARLEY TATE

HOPE STUMBLES

A POST-APOCALYPTIC SURVIVAL THRILLER

In a world without power, could you survive a brutal winter?

When a freak animal bite sends Madison limping through snow drifts to the cabin, the Sloane family's stable life is shattered. Rabies doesn't wait for sunny weather. Without a vaccine, Madison will die, but Tracy braves the cold to search for a cure. She'll save her daughter no matter what.

If danger comes out of nowhere, would you shoot first?

While out on a scavenging run, a gunshot pierces the frozen silence. Colt bolts for the street, finding blood on the ground and Walter missing. When his initial search turns up nothing, Colt must hunt the kidnappers down and save Walter before they finish the job.

The end of the world brings out the best and worst in all of us.

It's a race against the clock for both Tracy and Colt. Can they find a vaccine and Walter's location before the Sloane family is torn apart? Or will Tracy end up losing the two people she cares about most?

The EMP is only the beginning.

Hope Stumbles is book eight in the *After the EMP* series, a post-apocalyptic thriller series following ordinary people trying to survive after a geomagnetic storm destroys the nation's power grid.

Subscribe to Harley's newsletter and receive an exclusive companion short story, *Darkness Falls*, absolutely free.
www.harleytate.com/subscribe

SIX MONTHS WITHOUT POWER

DAY 190

PROLOGUE

MADISON

Clifton Compound
  Near Truckee, CA
  11:00 a.m.

"We need another wheelbarrow!" Madison wiped at a bead of sweat before it ran into her eye. They had been harvesting the last of the fall crops since the first glow of sun broke over the tree line. Corn and beans and potatoes. Late-planted carrots and the last of the tomatoes and peppers.

Peyton double-timed it up the row, pushing an empty wheelbarrow over the packed dirt. Sweat soaked his T-shirt like a football player finishing up practice. "We're going to be canning for days. There's more food than supermarkets used to have out here."

Madison nodded. The acre they'd cleared in late

spring had yielded a bigger bounty than any of them anticipated. They would have more fruits and vegetables and grains than they needed for the winter. She smiled as Peyton leaned in to help, rooting through the leaves for any stray peppers.

If a solar storm hadn't brought an electromagnetic pulse and threw the entire country back into the stone age, they would be doing the same thing right now at UC Davis. Fall meant harvest time on a farm or in an agricultural department of a college. She elbowed Peyton in the side.

"It's like old times, isn't it?"

She'd expected his usual grin and a funny comeback line. Instead, he stilled and his eyes lost their light. "Yes and no."

Madison's face fell. She didn't mean to dredge up painful memories on a gorgeous fall day. They should be laughing and carrying on before running inside for fresh lemonade and some of her mom's biscuits.

She risked a question that gnawed at her in somber moments. "Do you ever wonder about your dad?"

Peyton glanced at her with a furrowed brow. "Sometimes. But what can I do? He's either dead or living it up in some bunker in Los Angeles."

She reached out and squeezed his arm. Not knowing whether your only family was alive or dead had to be hard. But Peyton's father hadn't been a model parent. Every once in a while, Peyton still talked about the day everything changed. His father had cut off his tuition funding. He wouldn't graduate from UC Davis unless he changed his major.

Madison dropped her hand. If only his father had known agrarian skills would mean the difference between life and death less than a year later.

Peyton blew out a puff of air and leaned back on his heels. "Who knows, maybe the entertainment industry is thriving down there. Music execs always reminded me of cockroaches anyway."

Madison laughed and her spirits lifted.

"What's so funny?" Brianna appeared, looking every bit the farmer with a pair of dirt-smeared overalls and a bandana holding back her hair.

"Cockroaches."

Her eyes went wide as she stared at the dirt. "Where? You know I hate those things."

"Los Angeles, mostly."

Brianna's eyebrows shot up, but Peyton waved her off.

"How are the piglets?"

"Almost ready to be on their own." Brianna grinned. "Betsy's a trooper. I can't imagine having eight babies crawling all over me."

"I still can't believe you named all the pigs. Don't you cringe when your dad slaughters one?"

"Not really. They have a good life here."

Peyton rubbed his belly. "And bacon tastes good."

Madison elbowed him harder than before. "No tasty pork products unless you help me with the rest of the harvest." She turned back to the pepper plant in front of her and couldn't help but smile. They might be in the middle of nowhere and living like pioneers, but they were family.

As long as they stayed together, they could weather anything.

NINE MONTHS WITHOUT POWER

DAY 280

CHAPTER ONE

TRACY

Clifton Compound
  Near Truckee, CA
  10:00 a.m.

Fat, wet snowflakes landed on Tracy's lashes, melting into puddles beneath her eyes. Every few paces, she brushed them away and paused to catch her breath, struggling against the weight of snowdrifts and wind.

Two hundred and eighty days ago, the country plunged into darkness. No power. No internet. No cell phones.

The entire United States went from nonstop worldwide contact to an island nation cut off from everything outside. Through luck and determination, Tracy's husband Walter found her in the ensuing chaos. But safety lingered out of reach for weeks. The promise of a sanctuary cabin in the woods was more dream than reality, but thanks to Brianna, they made it.

Ten people, a scrap of a dog, and a feisty cat all crammed into the tiny compound in the wilderness of Northern California. Brianna's family had taken them in and saved their lives. Now they all worked from sunup to sundown ensuring they earned their keep.

It had been rough going at first. Warm weather brought interlopers and strangers hell-bent on ruining everything they'd worked for. But thanks to quick thinking and an arsenal of weapons, the Sloanes and their makeshift extended family survived.

As the stifling heat gave way to falling leaves and colder temperatures, the months passed with back-breaking regularity. Endless crops to water and harvest, supplies to inventory, chickens and pigs to tend. They fell into a routine of communal labor and the satisfaction of working the land. But Tracy underestimated the brutal, snow-filled winter.

With a grunt of effort, she resumed her trek through the forest. The snow sucked at her ankles and clung to her boots with every forced step. Hunting in December with a foot and a half of snow on the ground wasn't for the faint of heart.

Snot crusted and froze in Tracy's nostrils and she wiggled her nose to increase airflow. Even as late as October, she'd thought a place with food and weapons and comfortable beds would solve all their problems.

"The winter won't be so bad," she had told herself. "We have everything we need."

A clump of snow fell off a pine bough and plopped onto her shoulder. *How naïve.*

Apart from a vacation one Christmas holiday, Tracy had never spent more than an afternoon in the snow. Her memories of that trip were filled with steaming hot chocolate and snowball fights and rosy cheeks rounded with laughter.

Now a solid month into a snow-filled winter and the memories mocked her. Thanks to the cold, most of their prime hunting targets were hibernating, hunkered down, or out of the area. But snowshoe hares still hopped along their routine trails and foxes followed close behind.

With Walter's help, Tracy and Madison set snare traps in a mile perimeter around the compound and checked them every day. Most days all they ended up with were soggy clothes and windburned cheeks, but every so often, they were rewarded. A plump rabbit meant fresh meat for dinner and fur they could use for coats, gloves, hats, and a million other things.

The first trap came into view and Tracy picked up the pace, loping toward it with a clumsy, high-knee waddle. Although working twelve hours a day honed her muscles, it burned a million calories. Tracy's stomach rumbled as she pushed faster.

Screw guns and ammunition; food was the most precious commodity in this new world. She stopped a few feet from the trap and filled her lungs with frigid air. It was empty like all the others. With an exhale, Tracy checked the snare and the bait before moving on.

While Tracy worked the western side of the

perimeter, her now-twenty-year-old daughter, Madison, worked the east. In the past nine months, her daughter had grown from a smart, but inexperienced, college student to a capable and strong young woman.

Tracy wished it had been in different circumstances, but she was proud of Madison and all she had accomplished. From clearing land and planting a massive garden, to harvesting and canning and learning how to hunt, Tracy's daughter had proven that a positive attitude meant everything.

Using her teeth, Tracy pulled off a glove and wiped at her eyes. Burning tears coated her lashes. Next time they went into the city for a scavenging run, she needed goggles or oversized sunglasses. Something to keep the wind and glare out of her eyes.

After a moment, she moved on, checking the next three traps and coming up empty. Scratch rabbit stew from the menu tonight. She hurried on to the final snare when a shout stopped her midstride.

"Help! Mom! Help!"

Madison. Tracy ran toward the sound of her daughter's anguished voice. She cupped her bulky gloves around her mouth and screamed. "Madison! Where are you?"

She couldn't hear a response above the pounding of her own heart. Tracy stopped, heaving for breath as sweat beaded and slipped down her spine beneath the weight of her winter parka. "Madison!"

A million scenarios ran through her mind.

A hidden log beneath the snow could twist an ankle

or break a leg. A hungry mountain lion or bobcat could leap from a tree and try to turn her daughter into dinner. A hunter who strayed into their area could have shot her by accident.

Someone could be holding her hostage.

Tracy shivered and plowed on in the direction she'd heard the scream. Her side burned with lactic acid and her vision clouded with sweat and tears, but Tracy didn't stop.

I'll find you, honey. Wherever you are.

Tracy cupped her hands and cried out again. "Madison!"

At last, her daughter responded. "Over here!"

Yes! Tracy ran in the direction of her daughter's voice. Ignoring the pain in her side and the sweat soaking her shirt, she headed toward the last of Madison's traps. *There!* A shape in the snow.

Dark gray coat, flag of brown hair blowing in the wind, all ringed by a circle of bright red snow.

"Madison! Are you okay?" Tracy stopped five feet from her daughter.

The snow surrounding Madison ranged in tint from carnation to scarlet, all stained with blood. Madison sat in a depression, backside buried a foot deep, clutching her leg. She looked up at her mother, face as pale as the unblemished ground further afield. "I'm bleeding pretty bad."

Tracy scrabbled forward, landing hard on her knees a foot away. A series of gashes opened up Madison's pants.

Blood coated her fingers where she gripped her leg, steaming in the winter air.

"What happened?"

Madison forced a swallow. "A fox was in the snare. I thought it was dead, but it wasn't." She winced. "I bent down to release the snare and it attacked. I shielded my face, but it got my leg bad."

"Why didn't you shoot it?"

"I—I don't know. I wasn't thinking. All the other traps were empty. I didn't think I'd find anything and when I did, it looked dead. I just assumed—" Madison's explanation cut off as Tracy reached for her leg.

"Let me see."

Madison moved her hand and a fresh gurgle of blood bubbled through the cut in her pants. *Damn it.* Tracy couldn't make out anything with the fabric in the way, but the amount of blood alarmed her. If it was a bite...

"Did it look sick? Crazy? Was it foaming at the mouth?"

Madison heaved out a breath. "I don't think so, but it all happened so fast."

Tracy rolled her lips over her teeth. There were all sorts of rational explanations for a fox to attack. An injury, being cornered in the trap, just plain fear. But another reason flashed in neon in Tracy's mind: rabies. If the fox were infected, Madison needed a vaccine. *Right now.*

She dropped the small pack she carried and fished out the mini first aid kit and a bandana. "I'm sorry. This will hurt."

Madison leaned back and braced herself with her palm as Tracy applied the gauze. It would all have to come off inside, but at least the bleeding would slow while they hobbled back to the cabins. "Where's the fox?"

"I loosened the snare enough for it to wriggle free before it attacked. I guess it ran off."

A million worries flew through Tracy's mind, but she only voiced one for now. "The blood will attract other predators. Bobcats or mountain lions. An injured fox could lead them right to us. We'll have to be careful."

Madison reached out and grabbed Tracy's hand. "I'm sorry, Mom."

"Me too. Let's hope we have enough supplies to fix you up."

"Dad's on a run. He'll find what we don't have."

Tracy didn't respond. Their supplies were meager at best. No vaccines, no antibiotics. Did they even have a suture kit? The winter had brought more than expected accidents and injuries. She shook her head and focused on Madison. Staying out in the snow wasn't helping anything.

With a deep breath, she hoisted her daughter to her feet. Looping one arm around Madison's back, Tracy used her free hand to hold tight to Madison's other arm. Together, they started the slow and agonizing trek back to camp.

With every step, Tracy's worry grew. If the fox had rabies or some other disease, Madison might never recover. If not, alcohol and bandages might do the job, but if her daughter kept losing blood, she would be incapacitated for a good long while.

Madison winced and Tracy slowed. "Are you okay?"

"Yeah. I just need a moment."

"We can't stop, honey. We have to get you home."

"I know." Madison sucked in a breath, nodded, and they took off again.

They might have a small working farm and the privacy of a forest all around, but their situation was far from secure. No hospitals. No western medicine. No doctors.

Something as simple as a rusty nail or a sick animal could do them in. Trauma kits and first aid supplies could only do so much. Tracy hugged her daughter tighter and picked up the pace. Hopefully Walter was having better luck in the city. If not, they were in a world of hurt.

CHAPTER TWO

COLT

Mountain Way
  Truckee, CA
   10:00 a.m.

Why the hell does it have to be this freakin' cold? Colt hunched down behind the remains of a car torched back when the sun could fry an egg on the hood and he didn't have to wear a ridiculous parka with a scratchy fur hood.

He adjusted the sight on the binoculars and peered into the ransacked grocery store across the street. So far, apart from his stupid self and Walter Sloane, they hadn't seen a single person. Not that he blamed anyone for staying home.

Of all places for their plane to land on a trek from Sacramento, California to Hong Kong, it had to be Oregon. Between the landing site and Truckee, California where he now crouched, spanned endless forests, mountain ranges, and a metric crap-ton of snow. Not a single beach chair, tropical sunset, or gorgeous woman in sight.

If they'd made it all the way to Hong Kong, he'd be living it up right now: an ex-pat in paradise with running water, hot food, and lights that still turned on. Instead, he was huddled in the freezing wind, butt in the snowdrift, ten minutes away from freezing his junk into a popsicle and a pair of snowballs.

But it wasn't all terrible. Thanks to a chance run-in with a soldier and a tough teenage girl, Colt had a reason to keep breathing. Dani was the closest thing to a daughter he would ever have. Family made the cold almost worth it.

With a shift in his squat, Colt scanned the rest of the strip mall. The grocery store sat back from the road with a sizable parking lot in front and a handful of businesses on the side. Everything had been pillaged. Not a single window remained in any of the shops and half of them were burned into sooty-black caves.

He didn't understand what drove people to loot and destroy. Didn't they know what the future held? Instead of torching the running shop, people should have been loading up on shoes and gear. It wasn't like the UPS guy would show up next week with a shipment of new Nikes. Hell, FEMA wasn't even showing up with food or water.

Whatever was left of the government, it didn't stretch to the foothills of the Sierra Nevadas, that was for damn sure. For all intents and purposes, Colt, Dani, and the rest of their group were on their own. Which suited them just fine. After escaping the clutches of a crazy man and his ragtag group of defectors, Colt wasn't about to walk into another organized city and lay down his weapons.

Nope. They were off-grid and off the radar for good. Not that either existed anymore, but still. He was beholden to no one except Dani and a fluffy little dog who didn't have anyone else left. Lottie didn't weigh much, but she made up for it in personality. He'd trust that dog over a stranger any day.

Colt pulled a handwritten note from his pocket and ran over the list one more time. Pain medicine. Sutures. Antibiotics. Band-Aids. Gauze. Tampons. Bourbon.

The last one might have been his own personal addition, but it didn't make it any less critical. He could only stomach so much dehydrated venison and highs in the thirties before he needed a stiff drink to take the edge off. In a pinch, he could even use it for antiseptic.

In all likelihood, they wouldn't find anything. But every once in a while, a treasure would be hidden beneath the broken shelves and trampled displays.

Footsteps shuffling through the snow caught Colt's ear and he turned. Walter Sloane trudged up behind him, eyes shielded behind dark ski glasses and graying head hidden by a thick hood. Thanks to Walter, Colt was not only alive, but healthy, and Dani had survived more than her share of injuries.

Bullet wounds, cuts, bruises, concussions, and burns. You name it, they endured it. Most men would have taken one look at them and walked away. But Walter didn't. He'd remembered Colt from the emergency landing all those days before and welcomed him into the fold. Months of hard work later and Walter's age shone in his deeper wrinkles and tired eyes.

Colt nodded hello. "Find anything?"

Walter crouched beside him, hidden from the street by the same shell of a car. "Not a soul." He nodded at the grocery store. "Any movement?"

"None. The whole street is abandoned. We're too far from houses for anyone to hear us and it looks like this part of town was ransacked a good long while ago."

Apart from the grocery store and attached shops, a bank sat empty across the street, with a derelict building beside it and an express oil change place farther on.

Walter nodded. "The bank is empty. Car place, too. Nothing else is close enough to bother with, although I canvassed the two closest blocks."

"Then I say we go. The sooner we check this place out, the sooner we can move on down the road."

"There's a pharmacy a few blocks south. If the grocery store is a bust, it might have something."

"Agreed." Colt pulled off a glove and reached inside his jacket for a handgun, his service piece from his job as an air marshal that felt like another lifetime ago. The Sig Sauer had never let him down. He motioned toward the store. "I'll go first. You cover me."

Walter nodded as he readied his own gun, a pistol-grip shotgun loaded with six shells. It might not have high capacity, but no one ever had to empty an entire shotgun into a single assailant. Walter could hold his own unless an army came out of nowhere.

Colt eased around the car's darkened fender and hurried across the street.

The edge of the building loomed and he ducked around it, pausing to catch his breath. So far, so good. He glanced at Walter still crouched behind the car before sneaking through the shattered window.

Although the brick facade protected the inside of the store from the wind, it did nothing against the cold. If anything, the lack of sun made the air even more frigid. Colt pushed back his hood and his breath fogged as he eased down the far wall.

Thanks to the clear sky and the busted windows, Colt could reliably see half of the store. He tracked along the edge, past empty refrigerator cases long since looted of beer and milk. According to the signs still hanging above the aisles, medicines sat in the far corner, in the darkest section of the store.

Colt ground his teeth and kept walking, gun out, sweeping every aisle as he approached, working in a full 180 as he eased closer to the dark. By now, Walter should have made his way inside. They worked as a team. Walter watched the front of the store while Colt surveyed the back. Whatever he found went into his empty pack. If he hit the mother lode, they would work together to get it back to the Jeep parked securely in a grove of trees at the edge of town.

After waiting for his eyes to adjust to the dim light, Colt kept walking past destroyed shelves and crushed boxes of package goods and on toward the far corner. He reached the aisles for medicine without incident. They were trashed.

One shelving unit was ripped almost clean out of the floor and twisted over on its side, like Godzilla had smacked it on his way through the store. Another was warped and bent as if the entire local football team had used it for practice.

Colt squeezed between them and squinted. Boxes littered the floor. He tugged a small flashlight from his pocket and flicked it on. *Finding Nemo* Band-Aids. He snorted. Better than nothing.

He eased his pack off his shoulders and unzipped it before dumping every box inside. The shelves crowded in around him, but Colt kept going, shuffling through ripped-open boxes of gloves and torn bags of Epsom salt and glucose meters for diabetics.

Using the flashlight, he swept the shelves until a bottle caught his eye. He reached in, straining beneath the warped metal to pull it out. *Vitamin D.* Could be useful in the winter. He tossed it in the bag along with a bottle of kids gummy vitamins and a box of gauze. Not the worst expedition in the world.

Colt slipped through the last of the aisle and stood up. In front of him loomed the feminine hygiene section. Half a dozen boxes sat on the shelf, some broken, a few unharmed. He grimaced. This wasn't really his thing. But the list was the list and bringing Dani or Brianna or another one of the women along just because he didn't know the first thing about it was stupid and selfish.

He opened the pack wider and cleared the shelves,

sliding every box inside until it bulged and he struggled to close the zipper. All he needed now was the pharmacy. Like most stores, the pharmacy jutted out from the corner in a blunt-cornered box. Colt approached with caution.

The siding metal door was propped up, half off its track. Colt ducked beneath it. If the store was chaos, the pharmacy was a full-blown riot. Not a single shelf still stood. A fridge for antibiotics sat in the middle of the room, door smashed and hanging by a single hinge. The cash register was bent and dented, the drawer carelessly thrown on the floor.

Colt inhaled. Searching would take forever, but he couldn't leave until they made sure. Even one blister pack of Z-Pak would cure a nasty infection. Aisle by aisle, Colt searched, losing himself in the job.

Halfway through, he stripped out of his jacket and dumped it on the floor before holstering his weapon. Two hands and no gear would speed up the search. As he bent to read the label of a forgotten orange bottle, he jerked his head up.

There was no mistaking the sound.

Someone fired a gun in the front of the store.

CHAPTER THREE

COLT

Mountain Way
Truckee, CA
12:30 p.m.

Colt clicked off the flashlight and hurried to shove his things into the corner. A pack and parka would only slow him down. He pulled his Sig from his holster behind his back and gripped it with two hands. From back in the pharmacy, he couldn't tell if the shot was from a shotgun, a rifle, or even a handgun. It could have been anything.

He eased toward the metal door and ducked beneath it. No lights canvassed the back of the store. No shouts sounded from down the street. Maybe Walter found a stray elk or deer wandering in the road and took advantage.

The hairs on the back of Colt's neck disagreed, standing at attention like his world was about to crash down. But he kept the hope alive as he crept toward the light from outside. Over the last few months, whenever he'd expected bad results, he'd always stumbled across something worse. Maybe if he hoped for the best, whatever he found wouldn't be so bad.

Part of him wanted to run toward the entrance, but he had to take it slow. If someone else was inside the store, Colt needed to stay silent and invisible. He couldn't risk getting injured or caught off guard. He had to immobilize the threat by whatever means necessary.

Half crouching and half walking, Colt eased past each aisle, coming up on the cash registers and the front of the store. Pain lanced through his thigh in protest where a knife had stabbed deep a few months before. The skin healed with only a mild scar, but Colt's quad never regained full movement without pain.

He shivered as a blast of wind hit his chest. *Christ. I'll never get used to this weather.* Without his jacket, the front of the store would send the cold straight to his bones, but he couldn't go back for it. He needed the visibility and the freedom of movement a sweatshirt provided. He would just have to suck it up and hope the shivers didn't wreck his aim.

The front windows gaped ahead and Colt eased up behind the last checkout lane. He couldn't see Walter anywhere. He scanned the street, looking for any sign of life. Nothing.

Damn it.

Colt clenched his jaw and sneaked forward in a quick

crouch, skirting the bottom of the windows. He stopped five feet shy of the broken automatic doors.

In the kicked-up dust and snow in front of him, three drops of blood no bigger than a dime each glistened in the light. Deep red and glossy, they were fresh.

Colt crept closer. Too much disturbance to make out footprints. He turned toward the street. Another drop of blood, this time closer to the sidewalk. Whoever was injured didn't stay inside the store.

With a deep breath, Colt tightened his grip on the handgun and stepped over the debris. The outside air blasted through his sweatshirt and he shivered.

Scanning first left then right, Colt squinted against the glare. Not a single person. Not a flutter of fabric or hint of lights or even a whisper of conversation on the breeze. It was like Walter disappeared.

Had he been shot? Had he shot someone else? It made no sense. Colt checked his watch. One o'clock already. With the sun almost directly overhead, now would be the best time to search. But he couldn't do that without his gear.

Colt took a handful of steps toward the road and spun in a circle looking for more blood. There was none to be seen.

He frowned. Whoever was bleeding didn't just take to the sky and fly off. There should be more blood. Colt checked the road and other businesses again before crouching at the edge of the road. A set of tire tracks were etched into the fresh snow. Had they been there when he crossed the street?

Colt couldn't remember, but he didn't think so. How had he not heard a car? Did it coast into the road? Was it running barely above an idle?

A wave of shivers almost knocked him off-balance and Colt took a final look around. He would have to search, but that required gear. Rushing back into the store, Colt once again ducked into the pharmacy and tugged on his jacket and pack.

He zipped up the front of the coat as he eased back through the broken windows. Without reliable tracks or a blood trail to follow, he was hunting blind. Walter could be anywhere.

Colt cupped his hands and shouted. "Walter!" He paused and tried again. "Walter!"

His cry echoed and died in the street with no reply. Colt was faced with two choices. He could set off on foot and canvass the street as best he could, or he could head straight to the Jeep and cover more ground in a vehicle.

One was slow and thorough, the other was loud and fast. He glanced up at the sky and opted for a middle course: an hour of searching by foot before turning to the car. If Walter was holed up somewhere, hiding from mystery assailants, he would find him. If they were tucked away in a nearby building pumping him for information, Colt could ferret them out.

He kept those options in the forefront of his mind as he set off on a search. *Please let him be nearby. Please let me find him.*

If Walter had been kidnapped via car, Colt knew the chances of finding him were slim to none.

* * *

2:30 p.m.

Colt caught a bead of sweat with the back of his hand before it dripped off his nose. A solid hour of searching and all he'd come up with was a feral cat, a pile of empty PBR cans in an alley south of the store, and a sweat-soaked undershirt.

He leaned against the wall of what used to be a frame shop and inhaled. No matter how much he hated to admit it, he couldn't deny the obvious: Walter was gone. He couldn't believe the man would run off in pursuit of someone or something without letting Colt know. He'd have written a note or given him a clue somehow. Walter wouldn't disappear.

That left nefarious motives and unidentified strangers as the only rational explanation. Colt rubbed his face and pushed off the wall. The Jeep was three quarters of a mile away at this point and he needed to find it in a hurry. Colt planned to drive the street with the last few hours of winter daylight, searching for any sign of Walter.

Only then would he head home to break the bad news.

He eased out of the store and took off at a slow jog toward the south, hoping to reach the alley three buildings down without incident. First up, an abandoned restaurant. Vandals had torn the place apart, dragging tables and chairs out into the parking lot and setting them alight in massive bonfires. Only burnt scraps remained.

The next building housed a dry cleaner. Racks of clothes in plastic still hung in the windows, fluttering as the wind passed through the broken panes. Last up, the pharmacy Colt and Walter intended to search. From the front, it appeared secure. Metal sliding gates were lodged across the front doors and the windows were too high to climb through.

It would have been a good spot to investigate if Walter were still there.

Colt slowed. In the middle of the road up ahead, something caught the light, sparkling brighter than the snow. Colt crouched to pick it up.

A gold watch. His brow knit as he brushed off the clumping snow. How would someone lose this on the road? Colt turned it over and squinted. An inscription.

WJS: Congratulations on your retirement. Go get 'em, pilot.

A burst of air whooshed past Colt's lips. Walter. It had to be.

He slipped the watch into his pocket and stood up. The same tread from in front of the store cut through the snow down the middle of the street. The tire tracks were fresh; this time Colt had no doubt.

Without another thought, Colt turned west, ducking down the closest alley at a full-on run. The watch didn't guarantee Walter was still alive, but it filled Colt with hope. If Walter were conscious enough to drop it from a moving vehicle, it meant Colt had a chance. But he had to hurry.

Retracing their trek in from the edge of the woods, Colt crossed the next street and picked up the pace, running with his head on a swivel as he closed the distance between him and the Jeep. It wasn't impossible. As long as the snow didn't pick back up or turn into a blizzard, he could follow the tracks. He could find Walter.

Colt reached the Jeep out of breath and running on adrenaline. He started it up and peeled out of the cover of trees, intent on finding the trail and not letting Walter down. What took fifteen minutes to run only took three to drive and he turned onto the street where he'd found the watch.

The tire tracks ran straight down the road and Colt followed them, driving slow enough to make out any disturbance in the snow. Five blocks later, the tracks turned the corner and Colt followed. They joined in with a few older tracks, but thanks to the snowfall in between, he could still make out the fresh imprints.

He couldn't tell what make or model car, but based on the depth of the tread, he guessed an SUV or pickup. Following them led him a half a mile down the road. The tracks wobbled.

Colt slowed. Signs for the highway stuck up like green sentries to his right and the road widened to four lanes across.

He squinted through the windshield, but he couldn't make out the tracks. There were so many. After stopping the Jeep, Colt hopped out. He crouched to the left of the headlights, staring at the dirty snow. Tracks went everywhere. Some to the left, some to the right, some straight. He frowned. It was pointless.

Any one of them could be the right ones for all he knew. Colt stood up and looked around. The sun hung low in the sky, an hour before sunset. A handful of abandoned cars littered the gas station across the road, but otherwise, the streets were empty. The sun would set within the hour and searching for Walter without any idea as to his whereabouts could get them both killed.

Colt climbed back into the Jeep and dug around in the console. A single penny sat in the coin tray and Colt picked it up. Heads he kept driving, and tails he went home.

He held his breath and flipped the coin.

CHAPTER FOUR

TRACY

Clifton Compound
   Near Truckee, CA
   2:00 p.m.

It took three kicks on the door and a labored shout from Tracy for Dani to open the door to the main cabin. Housing the kitchen, dining, and communal living areas, it was almost always occupied. Which was a good thing today.

Dani pulled the door wide and her eyes followed, tracking the blood dripping across the wood as Tracy dragged Madison inside.

"What happened?"

"Injured fox. It attacked while Madison was checking the snare." Tracy grunted as she lowered her daughter into the closest chair. Blood soaked the bandana tied around the wound. Thanks to the long, arduous walk in the snow, Madison had lost a fair amount of blood.

Pale skin stretched across her cheeks and her eyes struggled to stay open. Tracy shook Madison's shoulder and she groaned in pain. "You can't pass out. Stay with us."

"How can I help?" Dani stood by the front door, lips pressed into a line.

"Find Brianna. I need her knowledge." Madison's friend from college wasn't a veterinarian yet, but she'd taken classes at UC Davis on the way to a degree. Before Tracy cleaned Madison's wound, she needed all the information she could get. Brianna might not have any, but it was worth a shot.

Dani nodded and rushed out the door, a blast of cold air filling the void in her wake.

Tracy squeezed her daughter's hand. The salty tang of sweat in the room drew acid up her throat. Foxes were usually scared of humans. Would the fear of being trapped cause a healthy fox to lash out? Tracy didn't know, but Brianna might.

If the fox that clawed Madison were ill, there might be nothing they could do to keep the sickness from spreading.

Rabies killed. So did a host of other illnesses and diseases. Tracy snuffed up the snot in her nose, now thawing in the warmth of the cabin. As soon as the acrid scent of Madison's blood hit her, Tracy covered her face with the back of her hand.

I can't sit here and do nothing. Waiting could get her daughter killed.

She pulled off her jacket and snow boots and layers of warmth until nothing remained but a sweat-soaked T-shirt and pants. With slow, careful movements, she did the same for her daughter. Madison's boots came off with little trouble, but she moaned as the jacket brushed against her leg.

"Just hang in there, honey."

Madison nodded and leaned back on the chair. "I'll have to have stitches, right?"

"I don't know." Tracy gathered all of the clothes and gear and set them out of the way before heading into the kitchen for towels and alcohol and scissors.

As she set the stack of supplies down on the table, the door opened and Brianna and her mother crowded in with Dani close behind.

"Oh, no! Madison, are you okay?" Brianna rushed to her best friend's side.

She managed a weak smile. "I've been better."

"Dani said she'd been attacked by a fox?"

Tracy nodded. "It was caught in the snare. She thought it was dead."

"I was an idiot. I should have shot it first to be sure."

Anne crouched down beside Madison and inspected the bandana. Brianna's mom was about her age, with shoulder-length hair fading into gray streaks. She'd been nothing but warm and welcoming to Tracy and her family ever since they showed up uninvited all those months ago. "There's a lot of blood. How bad is the wound?"

Tracy glanced at Brianna's mother. "I'm about to find out." With the scissors in one hand, Tracy pulled off the bandana and gauze before cutting away Madison's pant leg below the knee. From mid-calf down, her leg was a bloody mess.

Anne stood up and reached for the bottle of rubbing alcohol and a towel.

Brianna scooted into the space her mother left. "Is it a bite?"

Tracy took the supplies from Anne and popped the bottle open before handing the towel to Brianna. "Let's find out."

With a tight smile of encouragement in Madison's direction, Tracy poured the alcohol over the wound.

Madison screamed and jerked in the chair.

Dani rushed forward and grabbed her hand. "Squeeze my hand if it hurts."

Madison nodded as tears slipped from the corners of her eyes. "Thanks."

Tracy leaned closer. The alcohol helped, but it didn't remove enough of the clotting blood to get a decent look at the wound. She glanced at Brianna. "What do you know about rabies?"

"It's nasty, I can tell you that." Brianna leaned back on her heels, trying to remember. "I know that cleaning the wound is the most important thing. We should rinse it out with soap and water and then disinfect it."

Tracy glanced up at Anne, but Brianna's mom was

already on it, hustling into the kitchen for a bowl, water bottles, and soap.

"What else?"

"It's a long incubation process. Some animals are infected for months or even years before the virus reaches their brain."

"Is that when the symptoms show up?"

Brianna nodded. "All the things you see on TV—foaming at the mouth, aggression, stumbling—that's when the virus is in the brain. Until then, an animal might not be infectious. Their saliva might not have the virus."

Madison leaned forward. "I don't even know if it bit me."

"We need to clean it to see."

As Anne returned, she set a bowl of soapy water on the floor and handed Tracy a larger bucket. "Will that work?"

"It should." Tracy lifted Madison's leg and put it in the bucket before motioning to the bowl. "Brianna, you pour the water on the wound, okay?"

The young woman nodded and picked up the bowl, concentrating on not spilling. "I'm sorry if this hurts."

"It's okay. Just do it." Madison braced herself as Brianna tipped the bowl. The second the soapy water hit the wound, Madison launched off the chair.

Dani grabbed her by the shoulders and forced her back.

Brianna kept pouring. Little by little, the wound irrigated and the damage revealed itself. It wasn't a scratch. Not possible. From the puncture marks oozing blood, there was no mistaking it for anything other than a bite.

Madison must have seen it in her mother's face. "That bad?"

Tracy flicked her eyes up for a moment. "Worse."

"It probably wasn't sick. Rabies isn't common in the winter and I don't think foxes are usually infected in this part of the country." Brianna set the bowl down and leaned back. "But she should have the vaccine to be safe."

Anne looked at her daughter with a frown. "We don't have any. It wasn't something we could get without a prescription or a veterinary license."

"And we can't reach Colt or Walter to add it to the list." Dani let go of Madison and glanced at the door. "Should one of us go? We might be able to find a vaccine in town."

Tracy glanced at the time. Already four thirty. Dusk would hit soon. She turned to Brianna. "How long do we have? If the fox was infectious, how long can we wait to give Madison the vaccine?"

Brianna hesitated. "I don't know. My professor said right away, but we read a story about someone getting the vaccine two months later and being okay. It depends on how long it takes the virus to get to Madison's nerves. Once it reaches the brain..." She trailed off and Tracy knew what that meant.

If the rabies virus reached Madison's brain before she was vaccinated against it, there was no cure. She would die an agonizingly painful death.

She exhaled. "Do we close the wounds?"

"No. Leave them open to drain. We don't want to seal the infection inside."

Tracy clamped her lips shut to keep from cursing. She wished her husband were there. He would be able to make the hard decisions and go off in search of a vaccine right then without any regard for the consequences. Walter had a capacity to do the right thing even if it was a horrible experience. Tracy wasn't so blessed.

She wanted nothing more than to put on her coat and hit the road, but her daughter needed her to stay. There were no good options. Tracy glanced up at Madison. Her face was deathly pale apart from two little circles of flame on either cheek. Her eyelids fluttered as she moaned.

Tracy asked one more time. "Are you sure we shouldn't close it?"

"I'm sure." Brianna stood up with the empty bowl and Tracy lifted Madison's leg out of the bucket before setting her foot on a dry towel. The wound still oozed, but most of the bleeding had stopped.

Tracy forced herself to stand up and carried the bucket into the kitchen area.

As Brianna tucked the alcohol back on the shelf, she turned to Tracy. "Did you see where the fox went?"

"No. By the time I found Madison, it was long gone."

"Do you really think it was sick?"

Tracy glanced back at Madison and dropped her voice. "I have no idea. Even if it didn't have rabies, it could have something else. We need antibiotics and a vaccine."

"We've looked every time we've gone on a run."

Frustration raised the pitch in Brianna's voice. "Pharmacies are trashed, hospitals are worse. Even the warehouses have been hit."

"We don't have a choice."

Brianna shut the cabinet door. "Maybe Colt and Walter already found what we need. They've been gone two days. That has to mean something, right?"

Tracy opened her mouth to respond when the door to the cabin burst open. Colt stood in the entryway, forehead creased with dirt and worry.

A pit opened up in Tracy's stomach. "What's happened?"

Colt pinned her with a stare. "Walter's disappeared."

She gripped the counter for support. "What do you mean, disappeared?"

"I can't find him anywhere. He's missing."

CHAPTER FIVE

TRACY

Clifton Compound
   Near Truckee, CA
   5:30 p.m.

Colt shut out the darkness behind him as he strode into the cabin and closed the door. His neck muscles stood at attention, tight and strained.

Tracy waited for him to shed his coat before she spoke again. "I thought you were working together. How did you get separated?"

Colt ran both hands over his head to the back of his neck and held them there as he spoke. "We had a system. Walter gave me cover while I entered the store. We've done it a million times before. He's better with the shotgun, I'm better with a handgun. It makes sense."

He pulled out a chair and sat down beside Madison, registering her condition for the first time. "Are you okay?" His gaze landed on her wounded leg and Colt jerked his head up in alarm. "Was there an intruder? Is everyone all right?"

Dani spoke up. "She tangled with a fox in a snare. We're okay."

Colt leaned back in relief and Tracy bit her tongue to keep from pushing. Every second that ticked by increased her worry tenfold. At last, he continued. "I was in the pharmacy way in the back of a grocery store on the other side of Truckee, elbow-deep in broken boxes and twisted shelves."

He focused on Tracy and her heart thudded. "A shot rang out. I couldn't tell if it was Walter or not, so I hightailed it back outside. He wasn't there."

She swallowed. "Any sign of him?"

Colt hesitated and glanced at Madison. "A few drops of blood."

Brianna reached out to steady Tracy and she took the young woman's hand.

"I searched on foot for an hour, but couldn't find him anywhere. I was about to give up when I spotted something in the snow a few blocks from the store."

Tracy tensed.

Colt pulled out something gold and shiny. *Walter's watch.* She staggered back. "Walter got that as a retirement present when he left active duty." She remembered the party his fellow officers threw the weekend they moved. They made him open the watch in front of everyone. He'd put it on and never taken it off.

"Was there anything else?"

"Tire tracks. I can't be sure they were related, but I saw them outside the grocery store, too."

"Where did they go?"

"I hightailed it to the Jeep and followed the tracks as best I could. I lost them at a major intersection." He held the watch out to Tracy, obvious tension in his voice. "I'm sorry."

She snatched it from his fingers, barely able to contain her anger. It bubbled below the surface and flushed her skin.

Brianna and Anne asked a few questions, but Tracy wasn't listening. All she could think about was Walter out there somewhere, needing help, while Colt sat in the comfort of the kitchen. She jerked her hand out of Brianna's and stepped forward. Everyone turned to stare.

"You're telling us you don't know where he is, or who took him, or if he's even alive?"

Colt's jaw ticked. "That's right."

"Then why are you here? Why aren't you out looking for him?" Tracy's voice rose just shy of hysterical. "How could you just leave him out there?"

Dani stepped forward, hands on her hips. "Colt told you why. He didn't know where to look!"

"It's okay." Colt reached out and took Dani by the arm, but she shrugged him off.

"No, it's not. She shouldn't be mad at you."

Colt managed a sad smile. "Actually I agree with Tracy." He turned to her and the pain in his eyes deflated her rage.

"You do?"

He nodded. "We can't leave him out there. I only came back because I needed more people. I can't search for him alone."

"I'll go with you." Tracy walked toward her boots and coat, but Anne held out a hand.

"We should get everyone together and decide as a group."

Tracy sidestepped and reached for her things. "Walter's my husband. It's only right."

Anne leaned close enough to whisper. "Madison's your daughter."

Tracy froze.

"If Walter doesn't come back, she's going to need her mother. What about the vaccine?"

Brianna walked toward the door. "I'll go find everyone. They should be about done in the barn." She eased out the front door and Tracy stepped back to Madison's side. She put a hand on her daughter's forehead. It was hot to the touch.

As much as she hated to admit it, Anne was right. She needed to stay by her daughter's side. But that meant putting someone else's life in danger for her benefit. It didn't sit easy. She turned to Colt. "I'm sorry I jumped on you."

Colt nodded. "I deserve it. I shouldn't have left him on guard for so long."

Tracy waved him off. "It's not your fault. Walter's a grown man. He can make his own decisions."

The door opened and Peyton, Larkin, and Brianna filed in, followed by her father. Everyone except Tracy's husband now crowded into the kitchen area with expressions ranging from anger to disbelief.

Brianna shut the door. "I filled them in."

Colt turned to address the men. "We need to head back out to search for Walter, the sooner the better. I'm thinking three people and Lottie, too."

"Why the dog? Won't she get in the way?" Larkin found a spot on the wall and leaned against it. Career army, Major James Larkin spent a few months at Walter Reed rehabbing at the same time as Colt. They'd run into each other in Oregon and after a crazy few weeks, ended up together at the Cliftons' place.

Colt shook his head. "She's got an amazing nose. If anyone can figure out where Walter went, it's her."

Larkin raised his hand. "Then count me in."

"Me, too." Dani flashed a tight smile at Tracy. "I'm good in the city."

Brianna threw up her hand. "I can go, too. I'm one of the best shots. If he's in trouble, I can help."

Even Peyton volunteered, raising his hand as soon as Brianna finished. "I owe Walter my life. It wouldn't be fair not to go look for him." The kid might look like a football player, but he was all squishy insides and teddy bear emotions.

Tracy smiled.

That everyone was willing to help her husband meant a lot, but they couldn't all go. "Colt's right. It should be a small group. With Madison hurt, we need to keep some people here who can defend the place."

Peyton ducked down to Madison's side. The pair

exchanged a few words while the rest of the group broke out into overlapping conversations and arguments.

Larkin eased over to Brianna and waved his hand at the cabin. "You need to stay here. If everyone competent with a gun goes on this mission, the place will be defenseless."

Brianna pushed her unruly curls off her face and stood her ground. "My dad's a better shot than me and Tracy and Peyton can hold their own."

Dani spoke up. "Larkin's right. I'm not as good as you out in the forest, but I know my way around a city. If Walter's holed up somewhere in Truckee, I can find him and not get caught doing it."

"The girl's right." Larkin nodded in Dani's direction. "She's right up there with Lottie in the urban tracking."

Tracy frowned, but Colt stood up and closed the distance between them. He took her hands. "I know you want to go, but Madison is hurt. She needs you."

As much as it pained her to admit, she understood. "I know."

"Dani and Larkin are right. They're the best in the city."

Tracy fought to keep her emotions in check. Over the past seven months, she'd come to know the three strangers well, but they still weren't family. Relying on them to find her husband wasn't easy.

Colt gave her hands one more squeeze before letting go. "We'll leave as soon as we can."

Dani headed toward the door. "If anyone can find

him, we can." She smiled, brightening her whole face in hope. "Just watch, we'll all be back before you know it."

"Be careful."

"Always." Dani slipped out the door and Larkin followed. Colt leaned down to Madison and said a few words that Tracy couldn't hear. Her daughter glanced at her and nodded before Colt followed the others out the door.

Madison called out. "Mom, they'll find him."

She smiled at her daughter as a wave of tears filled her eyes. Willing them back, she pretended to busy herself with the discarded gear by the door. It would take all her strength not to follow the group to Truckee and help in the search, but it was the right thing to do. Walter would never forgive her if something happened to Madison because Tracy had been worried about him.

Tracy sucked in a lungful of air and forced it out her mouth. She had to have faith that Walter was alive and that Colt and the others could find him.

Peyton stood up and wrapped Tracy in a sideways hug. "He'll be all right, Mrs. S. You have to believe that."

She patted Peyton's arm and he let go. "Can you stay with Madison for a while? I need to get some air."

He nodded and Tracy bent to grab her jacket before scrunching her feet in her boots and easing out the door.

CHAPTER SIX

WALTER

Time and Location Unknown

Damp, clammy cold permeated his consciousness like dirty water seeping from a used washcloth tossed on the floor. Walter blinked, attempting to bring the world into focus. Nothing happened.

Eyes open or shut, the void all around stayed the same shade of black. He was either dead and trapped in some limbo of his own making or in a windowless jail cell in the land of the living.

Maybe another view will help. Walter rolled off his left arm and his hands slammed into the floor. He jerked against whatever bound his wrists and a searing ball of pain exploded in his right shoulder. Sweat beaded across his forehead as he fell forward once more.

Not dead. Good to know.

Scant memories of the moments before he lost

consciousness hit him in waves along with the pain. He'd been outside the grocery store, watching and waiting for Colt. The wind battered his face until tears leaked from his eyes and began to freeze in tracks down his cheeks.

He'd had no choice but to flip up his hood. But the parka's insulation muffled his hearing. No footsteps sloshing through melting snow. No tires crunching along the roadway.

Nothing until the bullet ripped his right shoulder apart and he fell face-first onto the ground. Walter twisted on the concrete, gritting his teeth against the throbbing ache as he poked at the wound with his chin.

Expecting a bloody mess, he jerked back when his stubbled skin found gauze. Someone cleaned him up and treated the wound. He eased down onto his side and exhaled as the pain lessened. Whoever took him wanted him alive.

What for?

He tried to remember what happened next. Snow in his nose and eyes. Pain clouding his thoughts. His hood hid the sun and muffled the noises behind him, but he'd sworn he heard voices. Were they shouting? Was there more gunfire?

I can't remember.

He closed his eyes and leaned back against the ground. He remembered spitting out bits of dirt and ice as he reached for the shotgun. It stuck out of the snow just out of reach. With his right shoulder on fire, he'd been awkward and slow.

More noise. A car. Something heavy and solid behind him. Was it a group? A single person? He shook his head.

Everything was a blur after that. Judging by the low throb in the back of his head, he could guess why. Gun stocks had a way of erasing memories and consciousness.

Walter rolled forward enough to rest his forehead on the ground. The floor wasn't sealed, and the cold and wet from the dirt beneath the concrete seeped to the surface. A basement? Warehouse? Fallout shelter?

He had no idea. Without more light, he wouldn't know unless he got up and felt around. Gunshot wound or not, he couldn't lie there and wait for his captors to come back. With a grunt, Walter used his head to push off and struggle up to his knees.

Still nothing but darkness. He closed his eyes and listened. A faint hum. Something mechanical. A generator? Boiler? Hot water heater?

It could be anything.

He sniffed back congestion and breathed deep. Moist earth, cool air. His bare arms pricked with cold, but he didn't shiver. Either the place had a heat source or he was underground. Root cellars and caves stayed temperate all year, but he didn't smell the brackish decay of living things long since forgotten.

Bracing himself for a rush of pain, Walter jabbed his right knee up and found the ground with his foot. Tipping himself forward, he managed to wobble and strain and drag his body up to stand. Vertigo rushed over him and he gagged on a rising tide of spit.

Walter gritted his teeth and swallowed. Falling down

wasn't an option. If he ripped open the bullet wound, he could bleed out and no one would know.

He closed his eyes and stood still, breathing in and out through his nose until the threat of fainting subsided. For all he knew, he'd been unconscious for hours. Lack of food and water and a gunshot wound could turn even the most seasoned of warriors into a liability. And Walter was just a middle-aged man who chopped wood and tended to a farm most days of the week.

Visions of his wife and daughter and the rest of their group filled his mind. He couldn't give up. Tracy depended on him. Madison was only twenty years old. Not that the current state of affairs lent themselves to weddings and college graduations and happily ever after, but he still hoped to live long enough to see his daughter happy.

Bending his wrists, he strained to reach the binds securing his hands. No matter how hard he struggled, he couldn't reach them. A tentative tug later and ensuing pain, he guessed zip ties. Uninjured, he might be able to break free. A few painful twists of his wrists and he could probably stretch them enough to get out. But with a bullet hole in his shoulder? Not a chance.

Walter sagged in defeat. Only after sitting for some time did he realize his wrists were smooth and stuck together. *My watch!* He'd worn the gold watch for years, only taking it off to shower and work out. Where was it? It couldn't have fallen off when he hit the ground. Did someone take it?

He grumbled. If someone on the other side of the

door walked in wearing it, Walter would make them pay. The thought gave him a surge of energy and he eased forward in the dark. With small, shuffling steps, he walked until his toe grazed something solid.

Walter turned around and his fingers brushed concrete. Not poured, but block. Keeping his fingers against the wall, he shuffled to the left. Nothing but concrete until he hit a seam. He repeated the procedure over and over until he'd circled the room twice, once at his normal height and once in a crouch.

All he found was a handful of concrete steps and a single door. Smooth, painted metal, and warm to the touch, the door was the only way in or out of the entire room. That explained the dark. Walter sagged against the wall and relieved the pressure on his shoulder from the zip ties.

He couldn't stay in there forever. Someone would come for him, and when they did, it could be the end of his journey. The door was his only option. He eased over to it once more and pitched himself forward until he could scrabble up the steps and reach the handle.

It slipped in his fingers.

He tried again. *Twist. Twist.* Locked.

Walter frowned. If he couldn't escape, then Colt was his best hope. He slid down the wall, sitting on the top step with his head against the door handle. If anyone tried to open it, he would feel it. It wasn't the best way to defend himself, but he would need to conserve his strength for whatever happened next.

* * *

A rattle in his skull broke through a dreamless sleep and Walter jerked awake. He blinked at the darkness, confused and discombobulated until it happened again: the doorknob wiggled against his head.

All at once it came back. The gunshot, the blackout, the windowless room.

Scrambling off the steps, Walter crouched on the other side of the door and sucked in a deep breath. *This is it.* Whoever was coming in would either end him or give him means to escape.

Fight or die. He didn't have a choice.

CHAPTER SEVEN

COLT

Clifton Compound
    Near Truckee, CA
    7:00 p.m.

The second magazine went into his cargo pocket and Colt zipped it up. They had already taken too long. Every minute Walter was missing increased the odds they would never find him. Colt refused to tell Tracy his fears, but the woman wasn't an idiot.

She had to know that Walter might never come home.

A knock sounded on the door and Colt swung it open. Dani stood outside the cabin holding Lottie and a wadded-up piece of cloth. "I grabbed one of Walter's shirts. I figure she'll need something to remember his scent."

"Good thinking. What weapon do you want?"

Dani chewed on her lip as she thought it over. When Colt first met the girl she was a skinny scrap of a thing, starving for more than just food. Now she was fifteen going on twenty-five. Her dirty-blonde hair had grown out past her shoulders and she could have graced the cover of any fashion magazine if they still existed.

Colt didn't wait for her to answer. He reached for the 20-gauge shotgun before handing it over. "You should have a pistol, too. Something for backup."

Dani nodded and plucked a small Glock 42 from the wall. Running into a Camaro at top speed had almost killed them all, but at least there had been a silver lining. A back seat full of weapons and ammo had been a boon no one expected.

Whoever owned the guns was out there, somewhere, but they hadn't found Colt yet. He hoped it stayed that way.

He bent to rub Lottie, the little Yorkie, on the head and grabbed the small daypack he'd loaded with water and energy bars and backup ammo. "Where's Larkin?"

"Waiting by the Jeep."

"Then let's hit the road."

They piled in the Jeep and in minutes were driving out of the gate and into the forest of the Sierra Nevada foothills.

Close to an hour later, Colt pulled over beside the grocery store. He'd circled the area twice, headlights blazing, looking for any sign of a person. *Nothing.* With the temperatures well below freezing, the chances of running into anyone would be slim.

They clambered out, Dani holding Lottie in her arms. Even with the little dog jacket and booties she wore, Lottie was no match for the elements. Keeping her warm would be a priority. If they couldn't spot a visual on Walter's whereabouts, they would need her nose.

Colt motioned Larkin over to the store's entrance. With his flashlight, he pointed out the drops of blood now icing over in the night air.

"Is this where he was standing?"

"I wish I knew. The pharmacy's at least a hundred and fifty feet away. Even if I'd taken off at a full-speed run, I'd never have made it out here in time."

Larkin glanced around. "There's nothing here but ransacked storefronts. Where would he go?"

"The question is where would someone take him." Colt pointed toward the street. "I followed a set of tire tracks that way, but they petered out just before the highway."

"If he was abducted via car, they could be anywhere."

Lottie squirmed in Dani's arms and gave a yip. The teenager looked up at Colt. "Can I put her down? She wants to help."

Colt nodded and Dani set the little dog on the freezing snow before holding out Walter's shirt. "Where is he, girl? Where's Walter?"

Lottie rooted in the shirt, snuffling up the scent for a moment before taking off, scampering down the slippery sidewalk in the direction Colt found the watch. The three of them followed a few steps behind.

It didn't take her more than five minutes to find the depression where Colt fished the watch from the ground.

"They must have been on foot. There's no way she could follow his scent otherwise."

Colt frowned. "Then where are the footprints? I should have seen some."

"Not if they were in the ditch. It's still all slush."

Lottie ran around in a circle, yipping and jumping on their legs. She was freezing.

Dani scooped up the little dog and held her out to Colt. "Put her in your coat for a minute. I have an idea."

While Colt warmed Lottie with his body heat and layers of insulation, Dani broke open a pair of hand warmers and shook them until the chemical reaction turned them hot. With Colt's help, she stuffed them between Lottie's jacket and her fur.

"They won't help her paws, but they're better than nothing."

"Good thinking." Larkin used a pair of binoculars to look around. He brought them down, frustrated. "I can't see anything tonight. The snow's bright, but the flashlights ruined my night vision."

Colt nodded. They were too pressed for time to wait for the morning. If Walter was still in the area, they needed to find him. *Now.* "Put Lottie back down. She's our best chance."

Dani did as he asked and gave Lottie another whiff of Walter's shirt. The little dog took off in an instant, down a cross street Colt hadn't checked.

As Colt stepped forward to follow her, Larkin

grabbed his coat. "I'll circle back for the Jeep." He pointed at a partially concealed lot across the street with an abandoned diner on the corner. "I'll park it there and hunt you all down."

Colt thanked him and hurried to catch up with Dani. She was following Lottie at a jogging pace down a street that transitioned from strip malls to warehouses.

He called out as he neared. "Where is she going?"

"No idea, but it's the best chance we've got."

Colt turned off his flashlight and motioned for Dani to do the same. If they were walking into a kidnapper's turf, advertising their presence wasn't smart.

The pair lapsed into silence as Lottie slowed down. Every few steps, her nose dove into the snow and she came up with a shake before trotting on down the sidewalk. As she neared another major intersection, the snow turned slick. Multi-story warehouses loomed from the edges of the road, casting exaggerated shadows and blocking out the weak moon.

"'This street doesn't get much sun. It's already iced over for the night."

Dani nodded. "I think she's lost the scent. It's buried under the ice."

Colt watched Lottie as she turned left and right and whimpered. He scooped her up and blew warm air into her boots. "Let's wait until she warms up and try again."

"No need." Larkin's voice caught Colt off guard. He'd been so consumed with Lottie and her abilities that he'd tuned out the sound of crunching snow. He'd grown soft on the farm.

Larkin stopped beside Colt. "I think I know where they are." He pointed down the street. "See anything out of place?"

Colt squinted into the moonlight, but Dani spotted it first.

"There's steam in the air! Up there!" She pointed at a series of rooflines several blocks away and finally Colt saw it.

"That doesn't prove anything. It could be anyone."

"It's the only lead we've got. Besides, what are the chances someone else is camping out in this part of town and Lottie leads us straight to them?"

"Maybe they're cooking up some backyard chickens."

Larkin cut Colt a glance. "Be serious."

"I am." He wished he could be as excited as Dani, but the facts were brutal. Finding Walter more than half a day since he went missing was highly unlikely. He'd have better luck getting struck by lightning. He handed Lottie to Dani. "Go with Larkin and put Lottie in the Jeep. She should be warm enough with the blankets and the hot water bottle."

"What about you?"

Colt pulled his Sig from his holster and ensured it was ready to fire. "I'll check it out, but don't get your hopes up."

"We'll meet back here in twenty." Larkin pulled Dani away and Colt eased off the sidewalk and into the shadows of the closest warehouse. His feet crunched through the snow and for the first time in his life, Colt wished he didn't weigh two hundred pounds. Dani's footsteps probably wouldn't make a sound.

He covered the distance to the warehouse in an agonizing ten minutes, watching every shadow for movement between him and the target. If the place was a hideout, it could have a sentry or a sniper on the roof. Anyone could be waiting in the shadows for someone like Colt to arrive. If Walter was inside, then they could even be expecting him.

Colt crept up to the side wall of the warehouse and leaned against the brick. Warmer than the outside air. Definitely heated. He kept tight to the building, grazing his back along the brick as he worked his way to the rear corner. It was old, built before tractor-trailers made deliveries and steel and aluminum were the building materials of choice.

At the corner, he paused to listen. A hum carried on the stillness, mixing in with the night silence of cold air and desolate, abandoned buildings. He crossed his fingers and wished for a window as he turned the corner.

He found one, but not the kind he wanted. Fifteen feet off the ground, the louvered single panes were excellent for cross-building ventilation, but terrible for reconnaissance. He cursed turn-of-the-century architecture and crept toward the back door. Solid metal with a massive handle, there was no way to open it without waking up every person inside.

Colt scrubbed his face and hurried past the door. The second half of the warehouse mirrored the first, leaving nothing but the front for him to inspect. From his vantage point at the front corner, a series of four windows, two on the right and two on the left, flanked a main entry door. Although they used to let in plenty of morning light, the windows had been long since painted a dull red on the outside to match the brick.

He couldn't see in even with the Jeep's high beams for lights.

Damn it to hell. Backtracking to their meetup spot, Colt hurried to a shivering Dani and Larkin.

"Took you long enough. Two more minutes and we were coming after you."

"It's definitely occupied. But I can't see a damn thing inside."

Larkin fixed him with an experienced stare. "So what do you want to do? Wait until morning?"

"Not a chance." Colt glanced at Dani. He hated to put her in danger after all she'd been through. "We'll have to go in."

Larkin's shoulders sagged. "Blind. With no information."

"Seems that way."

"I was afraid you'd say that." He swung the shotgun off his shoulder and exhaled. "Then let's get on with it. At least once we're inside I'll stop freezing my balls off."

Dani snickered beside him and readied her own shotgun, falling in step beside Colt. In no time, they were standing outside the rear door.

Colt took a deep breath. "Let's do this."

CHAPTER EIGHT

TRACY

Clifton Compound
   Near Truckee, CA
   8:00 p.m.

Every time Tracy snuffed back a frustrated bout of tears, the freezing night air stung her nostrils. She pushed her hood back and absorbed the cold smack across her cheek.

First Madison, now Walter.

Her daughter could be dying and her husband already dead. She'd gone from secure and stable to upended and on the verge of losing the two people who mattered more to her than anyone or anything else in the world.

Icy wind watered her eyes and dulled the panic threatening to rend her useless. Somehow, despite everything she had endured, a part of her believed it would all stop. *Surely*, the little voice in the back of her mind argued, *the country will struggle back to its feet. The horror of the past nine months will disappear into a worn and faded memory. It will all end sometime.*

Tracy shuddered. *I should take that voice out back and shoot it.*

The EMP wasn't a stumbling block that caused initial riots and unrest followed by crackdowns and order. Nothing got better. Everything just devolved. After the initial run-ins with the National Guard, neither Tracy nor Walter had seen any sign of aid workers nor any branch of the military. The government had been as silent as the radio.

Without electricity, the lights weren't the only thing to never work again.

Tracy wondered about the larger cities. Were they burnt husks of their former selves? Empty apart from a few stragglers who managed to scavenge to survive? Truckee certainly wasn't clawing its way back. The town was a burnt-out shell of humanity. Give it five years and it probably wouldn't exist at all. The forest would claim the tumbled bricks and concrete blocks and erase the American footprint on the land.

The collapse of the grid might as well have been a biological attack or a zombie invasion. From the way Walter talked about downtown Sacramento and Colt described Eugene, they suffered even more. She couldn't imagine what New York City must be like. Was that where the government focused their efforts? Did the major population centers scoop up all the attention and aid?

Tracy stepped off the porch and stalked out into the snow. With nine months of no light pollution, the fear of a pitch-black night no longer kept Tracy inside. The moon and stars—too many to conceive of—reflected off the snow and turned an electric-free winter into a natural night-light. With no neighbors for miles, they were alone. Ten people in a handful of cabins, working together and pooling resources for the greater good.

Could small towns where everyone knew everyone else be thriving? With so much of the country used for animal herds and crops, there must have been pockets of resilience. The Clifton compound couldn't be the only working farm this side of the Sierra Nevadas.

Tracy stopped walking and pressed icy fingers to her eyelids. *I've got to stop this line of thought.* She couldn't do anything about the collapse of the United States. She couldn't change the trajectory of the country or the downward spiral of even her own family into mere subsistence living.

All she could do was concentrate on their immediate needs: shelter, food, water. It was the best anyone could hope for now. Walter's absence tugged at her heart. Not hitting the road to search for him drove her practically insane. Combined with Madison's injury and the threat of rabies, she wanted nothing more than to accomplish something.

But Colt, Larkin, and the rest of the group were right; she couldn't leave Madison now.

What if something happened to her? What if Walter was already dead? Leaving her daughter alone because she tried to be the hero and failed would be worse than losing Walter. Tracy had to hope her husband was alive and that Colt would find him.

But it wasn't like Walter to disappear or to leave something as meaningful as his watch behind. That watch had survived everything from the emergency landing in Oregon to the escape from Sacramento and the years of ordinary life beforehand. He wouldn't let it slip off his wrist. Something bad had happened. She knew it.

Tracy exhaled.

She had to have faith things wouldn't get worse. It was the best she could do.

As she turned to head inside, a disturbance in the snow caught her ear. Was it an animal? An intruder? Visions of snarling mountain lions or bobcats filled her mind and Tracy dug out the flashlight in her pocket. She clicked it on and pointed the beam at the edge of the tree line thirty feet ahead.

A patch of reddish fur wriggled in the snow bank. *Fireball?* Could the little cat be out in the elements? If he were outside, then he was at risk of being caught or injured. Tracy stepped off the porch and hurried toward the animal.

Ten feet away, she froze. The pricked ears and black paws weren't attached to a fluffy cat with a penchant for field mice. It was a fox.

With a bloodied right rear leg, it had to be the one that bit Madison. Tracy stared at it. The animal bobbed and weaved like a drunkard, stumbling forward and back and never getting anywhere. Was it delirious? Weak from the injury and pain?

Tracy eased closer. The animal snarled and Tracy jumped but it didn't advance. Instead, it flattened its ears and pounced at the snow bank, attacking nothing.

A shiver rushed down Tracy's back. An erratic and discombobulated animal could be more than injured. It could be sick with a latent infection or Tracy's worst fear: rabies. She fluffed her parka up in the back and eased a handgun from the appendix holster clipped to her jeans.

Cold and unforgiving, the steel frame of the handgun slowed her frantic heart. Taking aim, Tracy steadied her breath and her hand and pulled the trigger. The crack of the shot echoed through the snowy woods as the fox fell in a lump in the snow.

Tracy closed the gap between her and the dead animal before crouching at its feet. Ice crystals melted into the burnt orange fur as blood from the chest wound spread out in a half circle. Tracy poked at the animal's shoulder with the muzzle of the gun until the carcass rolled over.

She pushed up the fur around its snout and used the flashlight to inspect the fox's mouth. No obvious foaming, but plenty of spit and spittle.

"Tracy!"

A familiar voice called out from the dark and Tracy turned around to see Brianna standing in the light of the cabin door with a rifle in her hands.

"It's okay. I'm over here." Tracy waved the flashlight and Brianna hurried down to join her.

"What's going on? I heard a shot?"

Tracy pointed at the furry heap in front of her. "It's the fox from Madison's trap."

"You killed it?"

"It was injured." She shined the light on the mangled rear leg. "It was stumbling around in a circle, disoriented and out of sorts."

"From the blood loss?"

"That or a sickness." She glanced at Brianna. "It could have rabies."

The younger girl stood up with a start. "Do you really think so?"

"It's possible." Tracy pulled the gums back again. "See all this? It could be some foaming."

"Was it super aggressive? Did it try to attack you?"

"No. It was confused. It snarled at the snow."

Brianna pressed a palm against her forehead. "I knew we needed vaccines."

Tracy swallowed. "Why don't you have any?"

"They're hard to acquire. I was hoping to get some from UC Davis as I advanced in the vet program, but I was only in the intro classes. I didn't get access to the lab until senior year."

Tracy chewed on her lip. Maybe it wouldn't be so bad. "What do we do? Wait to see if Madison shows any symptoms?"

Brianna stared at the fox for a moment before shaking her head. "Once she shows symptoms, it's too late."

"What do you mean?"

"Rabies is incurable once it presents itself."

"Then what's the point of the vaccine?"

"Rabies is a virus that's only manageable if caught before it reaches the nerves. With a bite like Madison's, it will take a while for the virus to get into her bloodstream and reach her central nervous system. It's that in-between time when the vaccine does its job."

"So if it's caught early, it's curable?"

"Yes. The symptoms we think of as rabies are end-stage manifestations, when the virus has reached the brain. That's why animals and people act aggressive and crazy. Their brain is being attacked by the virus."

"Before then?"

"Generally asymptomatic."

"So the fox..."

"Could be infected even without presenting symptoms."

Tracy swallowed. "How long do we have?"

"I don't know. A few days, maybe."

"Is there a test for rabies?"

Brianna exhaled. "Yes, but we don't have one."

Another bit of Tracy's hope crumbled. If they couldn't test the fox, then they would have to assume the worst: it was infected. "We'll have to find a vaccine. Where are they kept?"

"Hospitals, mostly. Some vet offices."

Tracy closed her eyes. They were miles from the nearest hospital and the chances that it had any medicines at all was slim to none. "What if Madison doesn't get the vaccine?"

"She could be fine."

"But there's no way to know for sure?"

"Not unless we test the fox and it's negative." Brianna glanced back at the cabin. "I'll get a jar and we can scoop some of the spit into it."

"But you don't have a test."

"Any vet office will."

"Say the fox is infected. How long do we have?"

"The rabies virus can spread very slowly. People can not present symptoms for months."

"But once they do—"

"It's too late."

Tracy nodded. "Then I don't have a choice. I have to find a vaccine."

"It won't be easy."

Tracy managed a tight smile. "Nothing worth doing ever is."

CHAPTER NINE

COLT

Warehouse District
    Truckee, CA
    7:00 p.m.

The screech of rusted metal-on-metal set Colt's teeth on edge. So much for the element of surprise. They were exposed. He fell back against the icy brick beside Larkin and Dani as the door swung open.

Half expecting shots or a grenade, he held his breath and counted to twenty. *Nothing.* Where were the bastards? Whoever took Walter wouldn't just let them waltz in and rescue him. *They must be hiding.*

Had he been spotted hours ago with Lottie? Were they made before Colt even saw the steam? He thought they'd been careful: no cars, no loud voices, no obvious recon. As soon as Lottie picked up the scent, Larkin trundled her back to the Jeep and they'd gone in quiet and close to the buildings.

It wasn't active-duty Navy SEAL-level of stealth, but they weren't bumbling around without a clue, either. That left one of two options: the operation inside the warehouse was sophisticated and organized, or so badly run no one heard the door.

Colt's finger quivered on the trigger of the Sig as he motioned with his free hand. Larkin nodded in the moonlight. It was now or never.

With a quick jerk, Colt ducked around the door, squinting as his eyes struggled to focus. Thanks to the lack of windows and thick concrete walls, he couldn't see jack. He eased back and cursed beneath his breath. "It's a black hole."

Larkin fished out a flashlight. "I'll light it up. You scope it out."

"Are you sure?" Dani voiced her concern with a puff of breath. "We'll be sitting ducks."

Colt gritted out a response. "We already are." Whoever was inside either already had them dead to rights or didn't know they were there. There wasn't an in-between. "We need to see what we're up against."

Larkin eased closer to Colt and held the flashlight high. On the count of three, Larkin clicked it on and Colt leaned forward enough to see. Disappointment dragged his shoulders low and he holstered his weapon. "It's all right. They're gone."

Dani and Larkin hurried in and shut the door before

filling up the space with more light. Folding tables in organized rows occupied the rear of the space, all empty apart from a handful of empty Styrofoam cups and wadded-up paper towels. Empty cardboard boxes big enough to stand in butted up against each other in the middle. The front of the warehouse held a row of cots, neat without bedding beneath the papered-over windows.

"What is this place?" Larkin spun around in a circle, shining his flashlight at everything in turn.

"It's a staging area."

"For what?"

Dani chewed on her lip as she walked through the tables. "I've seen this kind of setup before."

Colt turned toward her. "When?"

"One of my mom's dealers made his own meth in a place just like this."

Colt's eye twitched. "You think this is a drug lab?"

"It probably used to be." Dani scratched behind her ear. "But I can't imagine they have enough supplies these days."

Larkin held up an empty ramen noodle wrapper. "Looks like they've changed from dealing drugs to dealing food. I bet there's a fair number of people who would do anything for a cup of soup about now."

"Why would they take Walter? It doesn't make any sense." Colt walked up and down the aisles, shining his own flashlight beneath the tables and inside the empty boxes. "He didn't have any food on him."

"We don't even know if they took him. Lottie could

have been wrong." Larkin kicked at a cot near the windows.

"I don't think so." Colt approached the far wall where a radiator stretched ten feet across the concrete. He ripped off his glove and held his hand above the metal. "The radiator's hot." He spun around. "The EMP hit in March. There's no way this thing has been running since then. Someone got it working."

"Propane?"

"Or the natural gas line. This building is a hundred years old." Colt peered at the ancient tubes flecked with rust. "It might not be hooked up to electricity at all."

He pulled off his other glove and warmed his hands. "Either way, a person turned it on."

Larkin hustled up beside him and bent to check the knob jutting out from the wall. "And turned it off."

"But it's still warm in here." Dani's flashlight beam bounced as she shook her head. "No way they've been gone more than an hour."

Larkin agreed. "Whoever was here cleared out in a hurry. We must have been spotted."

Damn it. Colt hated to admit it, but they were right. If Walter was in that warehouse and they missed him because of their inefficiency, Tracy would never forgive him. Hell, Colt would never forgive himself. "That means we're not far behind. If we can pick up the trail—"

"We don't even know if Walter was in here."

"I think we do." Dani stood in a doorway tucked into the front corner of the building. Her flashlight beam bounced around the interior walls of the room. "Come check this out."

Before Colt could say a word, she ducked inside and disappeared. He hurried to catch up. As Colt rushed into the room, he almost tripped on a short set of stairs. They led down to a dirt subfloor and a room noticeably colder than the rest of the warehouse.

Dani held up a white rag stained in blood. "See?"

Colt hesitated. "That could be anyone's."

"Or it could be Walter's."

"What is this place?" Larkin eased down the steps and shivered.

"It's got to be a cellar. This whole area boomed at the turn of the century. Grain and cotton mills, mostly. They used the Truckee River to power grists and spinning wheels."

"So what's with the cellar?"

"Good place to store cotton and grain and prevent spoiling. It's cold now, but you remember the summer. A room like this would stay comfortable through all the hot months."

"And you think whoever was here turned it into a prison?"

"Or a holding cell." Dani showed Larkin the bloodied rag. "We can take this back to Lottie. See if she recognizes it."

"If they drove off, we'll never find them."

Colt crouched in the dirt, looking for any sign of Walter's presence. Tracking the flashlight beam up and down in uniform rows, he stopped at the corner closest to the door. "Come look at this."

He hurried to the corner, holding his arm out so Dani didn't walk over the words.

WJS Alive.

"It was Walter all right. And he's still breathing." Colt stood up and pressed his fingers to his lips. The man had saved him and Dani when everyone else was either dead or about to be. He'd argued for their right to stay with the Cliftons and even taught Dani a thing or two about ham radios.

Walter had become more than a savior in an uncertain time; he'd become a friend. Colt couldn't let a gang of strangers hurt him. There had to be a way to track him.

"What could someone want with Walter?"

"Nothing good." Larkin came over to read the words in the dirt. "But whoever they are, they aren't keeping a close watch."

"And they haven't tortured him."

"How can you tell?"

Colt glanced at Dani. "He was able to write. That means his arms aren't broken and he still has his hands."

The girl shuddered. "If they are anything like the men in Eugene, as soon as they tire of him, they'll kill him."

"Agreed." Colt headed toward the stairs. "Let's search the rest of this place for clues. Maybe we can find some evidence of where they've gone."

An hour later, Colt slumped against the wall. The

cold night air seeped through the concrete and he shivered. "We're never going to find him."

"We could bring Lottie and see if she can pick up the scent."

"She'll never be able to track a car."

Dani eased down to sit beside Colt and propped her rifle on her knees. "If these guys are anything like the dealers I used to know, they won't give up this space. It's close to town, has working heat, and they've gone to a lot of trouble to set it up."

"Then why clear out so fast?"

"What if we didn't spook them? What if they were merely done for the day?"

Colt eased off the wall. Dani might be young, but she made up for her age with street-life experience. "Then sooner or later someone will be back."

"Exactly." She turned to face him, the flashlight beam highlighting the excitement in her eyes. "As soon as they need to make another run, they'll be back and we can be ready for them."

"It could be days, weeks, even."

"Do you have a better idea?"

Nothing came to Colt's mind, but the idea of sitting around and waiting twisted his insides. Walter could die while they twiddled their thumbs. He tried to get in the head of a band of thieves or marauders. If they were organized, with a substantial base camp some miles away, then maintaining a processing facility in town made sense.

He panned his flashlight across the space. Was that

really what this was? He pinched the bridge of his nose. "I guess waiting can't hurt us. Let's get the Jeep and move it closer. Lottie can't stay out there all night."

"And we need the sleeping bags." Larkin headed toward the door. "I hope these chumps don't come back until the morning."

"Why's that?"

"Because even I need my beauty sleep."

DAY 281

CHAPTER TEN

COLT

Abandoned Warehouse
Truckee, CA
5:00 a.m.

Colt snapped awake and groaned. In the Navy, he always joked about his pregnant-woman bladder when he had to relieve himself every hour. At least now it had a purpose: no alarm clock required when he needed to piss before dawn.

Easing out of his sleeping bag, he passed an unconscious Dani and Lottie, both slumbering the morning away. He sneaked past with quiet, hesitant steps; they needed every minute of sleep.

Dani had grown so much since coming to stay at the Cliftons' place in the woods. She'd even given up a bit of her ingrained distrust. Colt knew she missed the intensity of surviving in the city, but he was thankful for the rest.

Thirty-something bodies didn't heal like they used to. He couldn't keep running forever.

He pushed the door open and winced. Colder than a witch's tit and not a light in sight. As quick as he could, Colt hustled back inside, shivering and rubbing his arms.

"That warm, huh?"

"Like a beach vacation."

He eased down beside Larkin and held his hands out to the portable stove. "How long have you been awake?"

"Since Dani poked me with a stick around two."

Colt counted up the hours. "If she can sleep until six, we'll have managed four hours a piece. Not too shabby."

Larkin pulled a pot from the stove and turned it off. The little blue flame flickered out and the heat fled along with it. "Coffee?"

"You have to ask?"

After pouring two mugs, Larkin handed one over. "How long are we planning to camp out?"

"Until these bastards come back or we figure out where they went."

"That could take a while."

"We aren't giving up. Walter saved our lives."

"Never said we should, but the longer it takes..." Larkin sipped his coffee.

"The worse the odds, I know." Colt rubbed a hand over his face. He'd grown so used to the short beard and scraggly hair he now sported that years of a clean-shaven face and military haircut seemed like a lifetime ago. "You ever think about Jarvis and how things are going in Eugene?"

"I try not to."

"How many other places are like that, you think?"

"Taken over by jerks on a power trip?" Larkin tucked his surfer-length hair behind his ear. Take him out of the wool sweater and tactical pants and he could have been right at home in Southern California. Not that there were any surfers left.

"Eugene can't be the only place."

"Walter described Sacramento like a war zone. Bigger cities had to fare worse. I can't imagine anything's left but burned-out buildings and dead bodies."

"Truckee's mostly intact."

"That's because everyone left alive froze to death come November." Larkin leaned back on his hands. "Face it. Most of America is dead or dying."

Colt shook his head. "I refuse to believe that."

"Want to take a road trip to find out?"

He snorted. "I'd rather keep some hope alive, thanks."

Larkin grinned. "Never knew you to be an optimist."

"It's more denial at this point. I've always been better at that one."

"Like when you insisted that knee injury wasn't career-ending?"

Colt thought back to their shared time in Walter Reed. Him with a blown-out knee and Larkin with a broken back. "What's the thing you miss most?"

"About before?"

Colt nodded.

"Comedy Central."

"I'm serious."

"So am I." Larkin gulped some coffee. "When's the last time you laughed at something so stupid it was funny?"

Colt thought about the time he forgot to wipe the rims of Anne's canned tomatoes and the entire batch spoiled. "Does tragi-comedy count?"

"Nope. I don't mean laugh-so-you-don't-cry funny. I mean real, honest-to-God, funny."

"About nine months, I guess."

"Bingo."

Colt rubbed his face. "When everything thaws, we should rig up a battery and a TV and go on a raid for DVDs."

"I'd give my left nut for a copy of *The Big Lebowski*."

"The dude abides." Colt snorted and drained the rest of his mug. "If you could go back, would you?"

"You mean before all this happened?" Larkin's brow shot up. "Of course. Wouldn't you?"

Colt glanced over at Dani and Lottie still sleeping on the other side of the warehouse. Before he saved the teenager, his life had been full of one-night stands and empty beer bottles. Now it had purpose. He had someone to look out for and keep alive.

"No, man. I wouldn't."

"Not even for that hot blonde in the rehab wing?"

Colt grinned. "Candie."

"That's the one." Larkin shook his head. "She had it bad for you."

"She had it bad for anyone without a wedding ring

and working parts." After another swig of coffee, Colt sobered. "What do you think DC is like now?"

Larkin whistled. "If there's any government left, it's there."

"You think we'll ever be back?"

"The United States? I don't know."

"Me neither." Colt lapsed into silence as he thought about all that transpired since the EMP. The fabric of society wasn't its morals or shared traditions anymore. It was the current running between the poles.

Electricity.

Without it, everyone was on their own.

He leaned back. "This new life isn't so bad. We've still got coffee. Food. Shelter."

Larkin smirked. "And I'm one hot blonde away from paradise."

Colt chuckled, but it was short-lived. While they'd talked, Lottie had woken up. The little Yorkie stood by the rear door to the warehouse, a growl rumbling in her belly.

He set the mug on the ground and clambered to his feet, Sig in his hand without a moment's hesitation. "Wake up Dani. I'll check it out."

While Larkin hustled across the warehouse, Colt crept toward the door. Were the thugs who took Walter back already? If so, they didn't waste much time. Overnight and back again meant an operation close by.

Thanks to breaking in the night before, Colt knew the door hinges squeaked. He waited on the other side, listening for any hint of the metal-on-metal screeching.

It didn't take long.

Come at me. I'm ready. Colt raised the Sig Sauer, holding it level with two hands. Still an expert marksman thanks to countless hours on the range to maintain his air marshal status, Colt had complete faith in his skill. He could shoot a pea off the top of a bottle across a field.

That old saying about doing something blindfolded with one hand behind his back? He might have tried it. Shooting an intruder square in the chest was child's play.

The door swung open and a pale face darted out from behind the metal like a rat on recon in a dirty kitchen. Colt advanced; a quick one-two-three shuffle. The kid didn't stand a chance. Before he knew what was happening, the barrel of Colt's gun pressed up against his temple and his lip quivered like Jell-O.

Colt dragged him inside by the worn-out scruff of his collar. "Who the hell are you?"

"Nobody. I'm nobody." The kid held up his hands. His fingers shook. Younger than Dani, twice as scared. "Don't shoot me."

Colt sucked in a breath. "Identify yourself." A bead of the kid's sweat rolled over the barrel of the gun and dripped to the floor.

"F-Frankie."

"Got a last name, Frankie?"

"Jones."

Colt eased up a fraction on the gun. "You part of the group that was here yesterday?"

Frankie's head rattled. "No, man. I'm not one of 'em."

"Then what are you here for?"

"I'm a scavenger."

Colt inched the gun forward. "A what?"

"Scavenger. Those guys are always leavin' somethin' behind. Candy bars. Cigarettes."

"What are they like?"

"I don't know."

The kid shied away, but Colt still held his collar. He twisted the grubby fabric in his fingers.

"Try again."

"There's a lot of 'em."

"When do they come? How long do they stay away?"

"I don't know!" Frankie whimpered and fingers twitched. "I'm telling the truth! I just wait until they leave, run in and run out. I don't stick around to get caught."

Colt spun them both around so he stood between Frankie and the door. He let him go with a shove before slamming the door shut. The kid had to know something. He was just too scared to admit it.

With a wave of his hand, Colt ushered Dani over. "Fish out something to eat, will you?" He glanced at the kid. All skin and bones. "Jerky and water."

"No freakin' way." Dani cut Frankie a glance and crossed her arms. "You just gotta rough him up a little. He's soft. He'll talk."

"We don't always have to be the bad guy."

She snorted. "We don't owe him anything."

Colt dropped his voice. "Let's give him a chance."

"Fine." Dani stomped over to their supplies while

Colt kept his gun on the kid. Frankie shrank into himself, hugging his hollow chest with his arms.

"I'm tellin' the truth. I don't know nothin'."

Larkin approached Colt from the other side of the warehouse. He zipped up his parka and motioned toward the door. "I'll do a perimeter check, make sure he's alone."

Colt nodded. Wouldn't be the first time they'd encountered a decoy sent to distract them from the real danger.

Dani returned from their gear holding a bottle of water and a handful of dried meat. While Larkin opened the door, Colt took his eyes off Frankie to grab the food. It was enough of a chance for the kid. He took off, lunging for the door.

Colt took aim. "You keep running and you're dead before your hand touches that handle."

The kid didn't stop. Colt swore beneath his breath and took off, sprinting to close the distance. As Frankie wrapped his hand around the handle, Colt grabbed his arm. He yanked, hard, and the kid crumpled to the ground.

Colt straddled him and kicked, rolling Frankie onto his back. With his gun aimed square at the space between Frankie's eyes, Colt put a foot on his chest and pressed. "Give me something or I take the girl up on her offer and practice my soccer moves."

Frankie's eyes widened and his face paled to match the concrete floor. "When they leave, they take the north road out of town. Across the highway."

"*Where?*"

"There's a farm. A big white house with three grain silos. You can't miss it."

Larkin opened the door. "All clear. If he's got any friends, they didn't come with him this trip."

Colt lifted his foot and Frankie sucked in a breath. He tossed the jerky at the kid's chest. "Take it and go."

"What?" Dani stepped forward, but Colt stuck out his arm. "He gave us what we wanted to know."

"That doesn't mean we give him our food."

Colt waited until Frankie scrambled to his feet and scurried out the door. "He could be an asset."

"He could be lying through his teeth." Dani palmed her hips. "He could be running to that farmhouse right now and telling them we're on the hunt."

"Doesn't matter if he does."

"Why not?"

"He'll never outrun the Jeep." Colt holstered his gun and motioned toward the gear. "Pack up. Let's get Walter."

CHAPTER ELEVEN

TRACY

Clifton Compound
Near Truckee, CA
6:oo a.m.

A gray wash lightened the sky above the forest as Tracy tramped across the hard-packed snow to the supplies cabin. Half an hour until sunrise and most everyone still slept, snuggled in down sleeping bags to ward off the winter chill.

Without fruit and vegetables to harvest and fewer eggs this time of year, the chores around the Clifton property could be accomplished in the daylight. Tracy wished Madison had opted for mucking out the pig pen this past week instead of checking traps. If she hadn't insisted on working the line, she wouldn't be suffering in the bunk room.

Tracy yawned away her fatigue. All night, she'd

stayed up watching Madison for signs of rabies. So far, her daughter seemed no worse than anyone with a leg injury. No fever, no uncontrollable sweating or mood swings.

She hadn't had the heart to tell Madison about the fox, but she would have to explain before she left. Madison would need to know the symptoms. She would need to prepare for the worst in case Tracy didn't make it back in time.

Tracy stomped the clumped snow off her boots and tried to send her negative thoughts along with it. Prepping for a trip required focus, not distraction. With a deep breath, she opened the cabin door and stepped inside.

The supply cabin housed more than just food and medicine; the small footprint also stored weapons and camping supplies. Tracy eased out of her jacket and hung it on a hook before setting down her small bundle of clothes.

She didn't know how long she'd be gone, but she needed to pack light. With Colt, Larkin, and Dani using the Jeep to search for Walter, Tracy had no choice but to travel on foot. The farm couldn't afford to lose its only other working four-wheeler if she didn't come home.

After regrouping from the attack on the Cliftons' place, Larkin and Walter had tried for months to find working vehicles in and around Truckee. It proved surprisingly difficult. Only older cars lent themselves to hot-wiring, and thanks to emissions standards and lease deals before the EMP, there weren't many around.

Add in a few months on the side of the road and even if they could open the steering column and join the wires, the engines wouldn't crank. They had taken to siphoning gas and maintaining the cars they had, instead.

Tracy exhaled and went back to work, picking out a small, one-shouldered pack that fit over her parka. It wouldn't hold a tent or a sleeping bag, but she could do without. Rabies vaccines were stashed in hospitals, not forests.

She stuffed a single change of clothes and two pairs of wool socks into a small stuff sack and rolled it to squeeze out the air before adding it to the pack. A travel trauma kit was next.

Unzipping it to check the contents, Tracy checked off her mental inventory: two pairs of nitrile gloves, EMT shears, a tourniquet, Sharpie, QuikClot gauze, an Israeli bandage, mylar blanket, burn gel, and a Surgicel hemostat. *All there.* Thanks to the Cliftons, Tracy now knew basic trauma first aid and how to use all the supplies.

She'd come a long way in nine months. Tracy zipped up the pouch and slipped it into the pack before grabbing a simple first aid kit and tossing it in, too. Between the two kits, Tracy could survive a bullet wound or a nasty accident and have a fighting chance to make it home.

With half a bag left, Tracy loaded up on mechanicals and defense. A backup Glock 19, same as what she carried now day-to-day, three magazines, and a box of ammo. Although the car crash that led to the deaths of most of Colt's friends was tragic, it came with the gift of an arsenal. Tracy would forever be thankful that something positive came out of that tragedy.

As she finished filling the pack with a multi-tool, flashlight, and few other odds and ends, the door to the cabin opened. The morning sun lit up Brianna's curls like a halo before she shut the door. "You're not doing this alone."

"Yes, I am." Tracy zipped up the pack and plucked her parka off the wall. "I'm not putting anyone else's life in danger."

"You'll never find what you need."

Tracy shook her head. "With Colt, Dani, and Larkin out looking for Walter, we're already dangerously shorthanded around here. If you come with me, that leaves only your parents and Peyton to hold down the entire place. It's asking too much."

Brianna reached for a shotgun and a box of shells. "If I don't come with you, Madison could die."

"If you come with me and this place is attacked, it won't matter."

"That's not going to happen and you know it." Brianna loaded the shotgun as she argued. "We've increased our perimeter defenses, the solar panels have full charges, and thanks to Walter's work we can see and hear anyone coming long before they reach the farm. It's as secure with three people as it is with ten."

Tracy shoved her arms in her coat sleeves. "I can't ask you to come with me. Madison is my daughter. You and your family have already done so much to help us."

"Madison's my best friend. I'm not sitting around

here and watching her die when I could be out there, finding a cure to save her." Brianna pushed a riot of curls off her face and pointed at the door. "I'm going whether you want me to or not."

"Your parents will never forgive me if you get hurt."

"They'll understand."

Tracy frowned and tried one last time. "We don't even know if the fox had rabies. This could all be for nothing. You should stay."

"And the virus could be racing through Madison's tissue right now, struggling to find a way to her nervous system. Every minute we waste arguing is a minute she might not have." Brianna yanked open the door. "The rest of my gear is with Madison. You should say goodbye before we leave."

Tracy watched the twenty-year-old stomp out of the supply cabin and down the hard-packed trail to the makeshift infirmary. Changing Brianna's mind would be impossible. If anything, the past few months of working the land and beefing up their defenses only made the girl more headstrong and determined. Brianna wasn't the type to settle down and enjoy the quiet life. She craved the kind of action they met while out on the road.

Tracy frowned as she followed the girl. Tracy would let Brianna tag along, but it didn't mean she had to like it. She thought about Anne waking up and finding her daughter gone and it filled her with dread. If the roles were reversed, Tracy would be consumed by worry.

After stomping her boots off on the porch, she slipped inside. Brianna sat beside Madison's cot on the far wall, their young heads almost touching as they talked. As Tracy shut the door, Madison leaned toward her.

"Do you really have to go?"

Tracy dug her thumbnail into her palm to keep from tearing up. "I'm afraid so." She smiled at her daughter. "We need to find you some medicine."

"The wound isn't that bad. We have some fish mox left. I'm sure I'll recover just fine."

"It's not a bacterial infection we're worried about."

Brianna glanced at Tracy. "Your mom found the fox. It was... acting strange."

Madison's eyes widened as she stared at Tracy. "How?"

"It was pawing the ground and snarling, walking in circles. It seemed disoriented and confused."

"That could be the blood loss. It was injured from the trap."

Tracy closed the distance and sat on the edge of Madison's cot. She took her daughter's hand. "Or it could be rabies."

Madison's face paled. "If it is—"

"Then you need a vaccine as soon as possible."

"If I don't get it?"

Brianna exhaled. "You'll die and it won't be pretty."

Madison leaned back against the wall. "How long do I have?"

"It depends on how far the infection had progressed in the fox. If his spit was raging with virus, then a few days. As long as the virus hasn't reached your nervous system, a vaccine will cure you."

"Once it has?"

"Then it's hopeless."

Tracy squeezed her daughter's hand. "I've heard of people living for months without symptoms."

"It's true. Sometimes the virus takes months or even years to reach the brain. But the sooner we get you medicine, the better." Brianna stood up. "You're lucky the fox bit you in the leg."

Madison tried to smile, but it came out in a grimace. She grabbed Brianna's hand. "Are you going?"

She nodded. "I'm going to help your mom. Thanks to that infectious disease class I took sophomore year, I know what to look for."

Tracy leaned forward. "We'll be back as soon as we can."

"Don't get killed for me." Madison's eyes shimmered. "Dad needs you."

"I love you, honey."

"Love you too, Mom."

Tracy hugged her daughter, holding her breath to keep from shaking. Madison wouldn't die. They would go on the hunt and find the medicine and come back home in time.

She pulled away.

"Even if you don't find the vaccine, there's a good chance I'm not infected. I still think the fox was just hurt."

"We can't take the chance." Tracy stood up as Brianna reached in for a quick hug.

The younger woman dropped her voice, but Tracy

could still make out the words. "If you start to show signs of the disease—confusion, fever, drooling—stay inside. You don't want to infect anyone else."

Tracy shivered. The thought of losing her daughter to a disease like rabies filled her with dread. She wouldn't let that happen. They would find a vaccine and prevent the sickness.

As Brianna gathered her things, Tracy waved once more at Madison and stepped outside. The cold winter air forced tears from her eyes and she wiped at her face.

Madison would be okay. Colt would find Walter. They would all make it home.

She kept repeating the affirmations in her mind over and over until Brianna joined her on the front porch. A warm glow lit up the eastern sky as the sun rose for yet another day.

"Ready?"

Tracy nodded. "Now or never."

CHAPTER TWELVE

TRACY

Unoccupied Forest
    Near Truckee, CA
    10:00 a.m.

"At least it's not snowing." Brianna wiped a blob of wind-induced snot from under her nose and keep trudging. Almost two hours into their trek and they were nearing the outskirts of Truckee.

It took concentration and stamina to hike through soft, loose snow. They'd barely said more than a few words to each other, focusing instead on not falling down or stepping in an unseen hole. But as the terrain leveled out, Tracy broached a topic she'd only touched on in the months post-EMP.

"Back in college, were you decided on a major?"

Brianna glanced up. "Not a hundred percent, but I was leaning toward veterinary medicine."

"Hence the infectious disease class."

She nodded. "I'd taken all the intro science classes and that was my first elective. Tucker was always trying to get me to try for med school, but I didn't want to work that hard."

At the mention of Brianna's boyfriend, Tucker, her voice warbled. It had been over six months since he died. A pang of guilt lodged in Tracy's chest. "I'm sorry. I didn't mean to bring up painful memories."

Brianna lapsed into silence and Tracy changed the subject. "The vet clinic we're headed to, is it in town?"

"No. It's a country vet. We took the pigs there when they were having a skin problem a few years back. The doctor saw farm animals, mostly." Brianna stopped and fished a map from her bag. She tugged off a glove and pointed at a red dot of marker. "That's our place."

Tracing a line down the hilly terrain to the flatter areas closer to town, she stopped at a rural intersection of a pair of two-lane highways. "Here's the vet."

Tracy guessed they were another three miles out. "Do you think a small vet like that will have the vaccine?"

"It's worth a shot. Farm animals are more likely to be bit by a wild animal than household pets in town."

"What about looters? Vets have tranquilizers and sedatives and all kinds of pills. In Sacramento half of them prescribed Prozac to anxious dogs and cats."

Brianna shoved the map back in her pocket. "Dr. Benton wasn't that kind of vet. He worked out of his house. If you didn't know he was a doctor, you'd pass his farm right by."

Tracy exhaled. Brianna was right; a country vet was their best shot. "If he doesn't have a vaccine, we'll have to head into town."

"The hospital will be the best choice."

Tracy grimaced. A hospital was the last place she wanted to go. "Let's hope it doesn't come to that."

As the sun rose above the horizon, the pair of women emerged from the forest and onto a road cut through rock and snow. Brianna pulled a water bottle from her pack and took a sip.

If they weren't loaded up with guns and ammo, Tracy could almost pretend they were just two women out on a winter hike, finishing up a week-long camping trip as they trekked back into town and the world before.

"Do you miss it?"

Tracy glanced up. She wasn't the only one stuck in the past. "Our lives before?"

Brianna nodded. "Everything. Electricity, transportation, people. So many people. I used to wake up and reach for my phone first thing. Scroll through pictures of my friends, see who was doing what that day. All from my bed."

"Now we're cut off."

"My parents had talked about what it would be like and why we built our cabins, so I wasn't in the dark. But I didn't fully grasp what it all meant." Brianna turned to Tracy and squinted against the sun. Any trace of the happy-go-lucky college kid she met that first visit to campus was gone. She'd aged ten years in nine months.

"At least your family had the sense to be ready. We

didn't even have extra food in the house." Tracy chastised herself for her foolishness. If they'd only had a plan for something like this, then maybe everything wouldn't have fallen apart. Maybe they wouldn't have lost the house. Wanda. Tucker. So many friends.

Brianna shook her head. "It's one thing to daydream and plan and can a bunch of tomatoes. It's another to watch the country you grew up in tear itself apart."

"We'll be forever grateful to you and your family, Brianna."

She waved Tracy off. "You don't need to thank me. Without you and Madison and everyone else, we would never be able to survive. We underestimated how hard living off the land would be."

"I underestimated how quickly the cities would fall."

Brianna ran a hand down her face. "We really are a bunch of animals now, aren't we?"

Tracy wished she could wave a magic wand and reset the country. "I still miss it."

"Me, too." Brianna focused on the snow beneath her feet as they walked. "But I don't miss the manufactured drama. Leave it to the apocalypse to show you how stupid selfies are."

Tracy laughed. "How about yoga pants? Those things are worthless out in the wild."

Brianna giggled. "Or makeup or high heels or..." Her voice slid into a sob. "Boyfriends."

Tracy reached out and squeezed her parka-clad arm. "Fancy shoes might be gone forever, but don't write off finding someone new."

"How am I supposed to do that?" Brianna looked around. "I don't see a slew of eligible bachelors just waiting in the snow." She sniffed. "Tucker was supposed to be the one."

Watching someone so young hurt so deeply, all because of a cataclysmic event they never expected, twisted Tracy's insides. For months, she'd fooled herself into thinking the worst was over.

The hard truth was that it would never end. She shoved the thought aside and brightened her voice. "Give it time. Maybe years from now, all the people who have found a way to hang on will come together. Rebuild."

Brianna snuffed back tears.

"In ten years, we could be back to civilization. We could have what we lost."

Tracy didn't push the issue and Brianna didn't respond. They walked, side by side in silence, down what used to be a road. Snow drifts had piled against the fence posts on either side and the women stayed to the middle, hiking on an empty highway toward what used to be a thriving mountain town.

The entire trek from the cabin to Truckee would be a slow descent down the foothills of the Sierra Nevada. She refused to think about the hike back up. As they came out of a bend, a snow-covered shape slowed Tracy's steps. "Is that a car?"

"What's left of one." Brianna pulled her shotgun off her shoulder. "Looks abandoned."

Tracy unholstered her Glock and lowered her voice. "I'll peel off. Check the field."

Brianna nodded and eased closer to the fence line as Tracy slipped between two strings of barbed wire and three feet of snow. Her boots sunk into the soft fluff as she canvassed the area. Nothing stood out. No movement. No tracks.

"It's clear." Brianna's voice cut through the icy air and Tracy made her way around the vehicle.

As she approached, Brianna knelt in front of a shape huddled beside the car.

"Did you find someth—" Tracy froze. It wasn't a bush or a pile of discarded gear. The shape nestled beside the front fender of an ice-covered Honda used to be human.

Brianna reached out and dusted the snow away. A woman's blue face emerged. Eyes closed, head resting on the shoulder of a man. While Tracy watched, Brianna uncovered the rest of their bodies.

Two people sitting on the side of the road, turned to ice. The man had his arm around the woman, and they were huddled together like somehow their puny body heat would make up for temperatures in the teens.

Brianna backed up in disgust. "Why didn't they stay in the car? Or keep moving? Sitting out here, they were exposed. Just waiting for winter to claim them."

Tracy crouched in front of the woman. Thanks to the brutal winds and months of snow, she couldn't make out more than her shape. What was she in a prior life? A teacher? Secretary? Biochemist? What was her life story? Why did it end in the middle of nowhere on the side of the road?

Her head sagged and Tracy focused on the woman's hands. They clasped a piece of paper. Tracy leaned forward and brushed off the snow. *Is it a photo?* She tugged at it with her gloved hand. Ice cracked and splintered. She yanked harder and the paper tore at the edge and came free. She stood up and brushed off the snow.

It was a photograph of a little girl. No older than ten, she looked a lot like Madison all those years ago. Brown hair, freckles across her nose, braces on her teeth. Smile full of light and life and an unblemished childhood. A snapshot of a time that seemed so long ago.

Tracy swallowed. "Any sign of a girl?"

Brianna scraped snow off the window of the car and cupped her hands around her face to peer inside. "It's empty."

"We need to make sure." Tracy held a little bead of hope in her heart even though she knew it was pointless. The couple had been dead for days if not weeks. They could have succumbed to the cold back when the first snowfall landed in November, waiting for someone to find them ever since.

But Tracy persevered, searching the area and kicking at clumps of snow until satisfied the child wasn't there. She set the photograph in the dead woman's lap.

"You still think in ten years we'll rebuild?" Brianna's voice cut like the wind.

Tracy swallowed.

"In ten years, how many people will even be left?"

Tracy fought against the despair. "The girl might still be alive. Maybe she's somewhere safe and warm."

Brianna slung her shotgun over her shoulder and turned to the road. "For her sake, I hope she's dead."

CHAPTER THIRTEEN

COLT

Unidentified Farm
  Near Truckee, CA
  11:00 a.m.

"I'm sick of waiting." Dani fidgeted beside Colt in the Jeep. "I say we hit them now when they aren't expecting us, find Walter, and get out."

Colt put the binoculars down with a sigh. "We can't go guns blazing without a plan or any evidence that Walter's inside. For all we know the kid was lying and this is a trap."

"I thought that's what I said." She crossed her arms in a huff.

Colt frowned. He'd already busted into the warehouse without a plan or any eyes on the inside. They were lucky that time. No telling whether they'd be lucky again. The odds weren't in their favor.

He leaned toward Dani. "You may be right, but that doesn't mean we either ignore it or just rush in. I reconned the crap out of Jarvis and that apartment before I broke in and it worked. If I'd just rushed in, who knows where we'd be by now."

"In a dumpster, being eaten by flies, probably." Larkin adjusted his position and picked up his binoculars. "We do this right or we don't do it. This isn't like the warehouse with only one way in and a limited time horizon. Look at this place."

After they had packed up their gear, it took an hour to find the place Frankie described. Sitting by the Truckee River in a small valley-shaped clearing, the three silos stood out like giant mushrooms in the snow. Colt had pulled the Jeep into the forest on the ridge above, far enough away to avoid detection, and found a place to camp out behind a grove of young pines.

For the past two hours, Colt had watched the farm through binoculars. From the distance, he couldn't make out faces or confirm identities, but what he saw, he didn't like. He turned to Larkin in the passenger seat. "It appears to be a fully-functioning farm. There's open areas that must be plowed fields and barns locked up tight."

Larkin leaned back. "Until we get a visual on Walter, we can't go in there. We could be shooting up innocent civilians."

"I could go in and pretend to be lost." Excitement crept into Dani's voice from the back seat. "Then you all could sneak in undetected."

"Not a chance." Colt wasn't about to use her as a decoy. Not this time. "We wait until we see Walter with our own eyes or we don't go in."

"Fine." Dani flopped back and crossed her arms and Colt clamped his lips shut to keep from grinning.

Despite her bravado and capability with a gun, Dani was still a teenager at heart. He tried not to tease her when it showed. Instead, he met her pouty eyes in the mirror. "How about you get some sleep? We might be up all night."

Dani made a show of fluffing her sleeping bag into a pillow before curling up on the seat. "Wake me up when you get sick of doing nothing."

As Colt turned around, Lottie squirmed past him and found the hollow between Dani's chest and knees. Both fell asleep within minutes.

Colt picked up the binoculars as snoring rose from the back seat. He tried to think about what would be happening back home around this time. Anne would be readying lunch. Brianna would be coming in from the barns with empty feed pails and covered in straw from the animals. Tracy and Madison would be cleaning any animals caught overnight in the traps. The men would be splitting wood or inventorying weapons or out on a run.

There should be some activity below him, but so far he hadn't seen much. As he waited a barn door opened. A single figure came out carrying something in his arms. From the distance, Colt couldn't make out what it was.

He thought about Dani's comments and her push to hit the farm. The girl had a point. Walter could be tied up in a basement or being tortured as they sat there and waited.

What if his hesitation caused Walter's death? Colt glanced at Larkin, but the former soldier shook his head. "Your instincts are solid. We shouldn't go in without visual confirmation."

"And if that gets him killed?" Colt ran a hand down his face. "It'll be my fault. I left him outside that store while I took my sweet time inside."

"If the roles were reversed, would he have done the same thing?"

"Maybe." But Colt still felt responsible. He couldn't wait anymore. "We've hung back long enough. I'm going closer for some on-foot recon. We're not getting the job done up here."

Larkin glanced at the back seat. "Two of us could cover twice as much ground."

Colt shook his head. "I'll go alone. If I'm not back in an hour or two, wake Dani up and see if you can get some sleep. You might need it."

He pushed his way out of the Jeep and shivered. According to Brianna's family, this first winter without nationwide electricity had been a beast. Highs below normal, more snowfall than usual. It didn't take a TV weatherman to tell Colt the next few months would be a challenge.

With only a thin glove on his shooting hand, Colt held his pistol low and eased into the forest. He'd parked the Jeep behind a solid stand of evergreen bushes at a vantage point well north of the farm. With bright yellow paint, it wasn't a vehicle meant for stealth operations. Any serious reconnaissance would need to be on foot.

Colt tugged his zipper up and snugged down his skull cap. His ears would need to freeze to listen for anyone coming. A farm this size might have sentries or roving security. He couldn't risk being seen.

The snow hampered his efforts. In the fall or summer, he could creep through the forest like a shadow and come right up on someone before they even knew he was there. But in the winter he might as well paint a giant red bullseye on his chest. Hard to conceal a two-hundred-pound man in a dark gray parka against glaring snow.

He planned every step. Creep behind this tree, dart to that bush, use that rock as cover. Edging down the hillside, it took Colt well over an hour to reach a safe vantage point. An outcropping of rock free from snow gave him enough cover to rest.

His breath blew out in thick clouds and he waited, crouched behind the warmed granite until he could control his breathing. Only then did he inch onto the top of the boulder and bring his binoculars into focus.

Whoa. First impressions could be deceiving, but Colt wasn't prepared for the scale of the place. From a thousand yards back, it seemed large but manageable. Up close, the operation was massive. Not just one field for crops, but three ringed the central barn. Fencing separated pens for animals. Multiple barns clustered around the largest open area. The silos dwarfed even the tallest pine.

Big enough to shelter horses in the winter, the largest

barn could be full of stables or vehicles or an entire army. The smaller ones could house pigs or sheep or a sizable flock of chickens. The Clifton place took ten people working around the clock to maintain; this place could easily need thirty.

As he shifted position on the rock, a side door to the largest barn slid open. Two men emerged, each holding a rifle with a scope. Colt's breath caught. With scopes, they could spot him. He was close enough to be a viable target. *Shit.*

He pressed closer to the rock, willing his parka and knit cap to blend in. One thing he'd learned while on active duty was that staying still was the best way to stay alive. The military equivalent of hug-a-tree for lost kids.

Colt kept watching. The two men shared a smoke a few yards from the barn, puffing clouds into the air. A short laugh carried up the hill.

With relaxed shoulders and guns leaned at ease, neither man was concerned or afraid. Either they didn't have Walter or he wasn't a threat. Colt frowned and kept watching. The pair of men finished their smoke and retreated to the door. He almost wished they would head out on patrol so he could pick them off. A captured sentry might give him all the info he needed.

The door to the barn opened, but the men didn't go inside. Instead, they ushered someone out. Colt rose up and adjusted the binoculars. *Walter!*

One man wrapped a hand around his upper arm and led him out of the barn. The other man followed behind with his rifle pointed at the ground, but ready.

Colt squinted. A parka was draped over Walter's shoulders as if he were a football player staying warm on the sidelines. His hands were clasped in front of him.

Restraints? Handcuffs? Colt couldn't tell for sure. He watched as the threesome stopped at the nearest tree line. Colt snorted. They were letting him take a piss. *At least he's not stuck in his own filth.* After he finished, the man with one hand on Walter spun him around and Colt got a first good look at his friend.

A bruise colored his forehead purple, but other than that, he appeared fine. No anguish on his face. No confusion or agitation as he walked back to the barn. The guard keeping up the rear rushed forward, slid open the door, and Walter and the men disappeared.

Colt lowered the binoculars and took a deep breath. *Walter is alive.* Relief coursed through Colt's veins. Ever since he saw the droplets of blood in the snow, he feared the worst. His optimism had faded by the minute, but thanks to Lottie and a chance encounter with Frankie, they found one of their own.

Now came the hard part: breaking him out. Colt eased off the rock and sat with his back to the farm. Finally a job he could handle. It had been months since he'd used any of his skills. He hadn't even been able to shoot as much as he liked to maintain his proficiency. Ammunition was a finite resource now.

He sucked in a lungful of cold air. His newfound farming skills could take a back seat for the next twenty-four hours. Colt had a mission. He cracked his knuckles and checked the time. One thirty in the afternoon. Plenty of time to prepare.

By the time night fell, they would be ready. With any luck, by the morning they would be driving into the Clifton compound, ready to reunite a family. He crept back into the cover of the trees.

CHAPTER FOURTEEN

TRACY

Woodland Veterinary Services
Truckee, CA
4:30 p.m.

In the middle of winter, the sun set so early it caught Tracy off guard. She'd hoped to make it to the vet, find a vaccine, and be halfway home by now. But thanks to the snow and a steep descent, it took them all day to reach the outskirts of town. Declining in elevation from seven thousand to five thousand feet didn't seem like much in the abstract, but in reality it was a brutish slog. The hike up would be worse.

No matter how much she wished for the Jeep, they had to keep going. Madison depended on her. The sunlight waned behind them, barely edging over the trees. Within half an hour it would be difficult to see. An hour would bring on darkness.

Brianna pushed her hood off her face and squinted into the impending dusk. "There it is." She pointed at a speck of a house, white clapboard blending in with the snow all around.

"Are you sure? It doesn't look like a vet. It looks like a farm."

"That's why I thought of it. Dr. Benton didn't advertise. If you didn't know him, he didn't see you or your animals."

Tracy grimaced. A vet without a sign who worked out of his house didn't instill her with confidence, but she pushed the doubts aside. They needed to get in and get out without any drama.

"Let's loop it, make sure it's clear, then we can head in."

Together, the women walked the edge of the property, skirting a fence line and the worst of the snowdrifts. It collected against any barrier, piling up like confetti in gutters after a parade. The house hugged the southeastern corner of the property, with a barn out back and a lump of something that could have been a car in the drive.

"There are no tire tracks or footprints anywhere. Are you sure he didn't retire?"

Brianna shrugged. "He was still here a month or so before the power went out. Maybe he packed up and left after."

"What about the vaccines? Don't they need to be kept cold?"

Brianna shivered. "I don't think that's a problem

right now."

Tracy bit the inside of her cheek. The temperatures in the foothills didn't reach the triple digits of Sacramento, but it still warmed into the low eighties. Left exposed, would a round of vaccinations even be effective? She shoved the thoughts aside. Even a less-potent vaccine was better than nothing.

She eased closer to the house. "I'll try and get in."

Brianna checked her shotgun. "I'll stand watch."

Tracy pulled off her gloves as she walked up to the front door. She wasn't as skilled as her husband at picking locks, but he'd taught her the basics last time they were out on a supply run. The metal skewers he found in a ransacked dollar store were better than any bobby pin.

Using her left hand to hold one skewer low in the lock, Tracy used her right hand to jiggle the tines. Up and down she worked the loose skewer, straining to hear the lock fall into place.

The cold wasn't helping. With a deep breath, she tried again. Tracy leaned closer, struggling to see in the fading sunlight. Frustration gnawed at her, but she pushed it back. Walter was missing and Madison was injured. If she didn't get into this vet's office, what hope did she have to keep going?

I might be the only Sloane left. The thought shoved her back on her heels and a skewer fell from the lock and landed in the snow.

I've been so complacent and lazy. All those summer months when the harvest came in easy and laughter filled the cabins. She'd discounted winter and bad weather and freak accidents. Other people who might want to do them harm. It hadn't been that long since a crew tried to take what they had. But she'd let the repetitive days and the hard work lull her into a false sense of security.

Tracy shoved her hand in the snow, digging for the now-frozen bit of metal.

Crunching footsteps sounded behind her and Tracy turned around. "I can't get it open."

Brianna hoisted a hunk of rock in her gloved hand. "Then we get in another way. I'm too cold to wait out here any longer." She pulled back like a shot-put champ and heaved the rock at the door's window.

The glass shattered and Brianna reached her arm inside. She unlocked the door from the inside and pulled it open.

Tracy stared at her for a moment.

"What? I'm surprised someone hasn't done it already." The younger woman stepped into the dark. "You coming?"

Brianna's flashlight flicked on as Tracy eased inside. Dust and stale air and the stink of animals dead and long past rotting filled her nose. She used a glove to block the worst of the smell.

"Did he board animals here?"

"I can't imagine that many locals needed a place to keep their chickens while they went on vacation." Brianna canvassed the lobby with the flashlight.

Plastic chairs. Peeling linoleum. Stained wallpaper. The place had seen better days.

"Did it always look like this?"

"Dr. Benton didn't win you over with style, but he also took all comers. People down on their luck, local farmers, anyone." Brianna pointed toward a door. "Medicine should all be in the back through here."

Tracy pulled her main weapon from her holster before clicking on her own flashlight. She held them in a cross in front of her like her husband instructed. "How old was he?"

"Ancient." Brianna pushed the door open. The smell intensified.

Tracy gagged. "Whatever animals he kept in here, they've been dead and shut up a long time."

"We'll have to search the whole space. I never came back here."

Occupying no more than a few hundred square feet, the vet seemed more like a prep space for a home business than a hospital. Cabinets ran across two walls and an oversized exam table sat in the middle.

They worked as a team, Tracy shining her light while Brianna opened doors and peered inside. First aid supplies, shampoo, nail clippers, boxes of flea and tick preventive, but no medicine.

Tracy slowed. They were going about it all wrong. "Everyone knows vets keep medicines on hand, right?"

Brianna snorted. "That's why we're here."

"But it's not just vaccines, it's all sorts of things. Antibiotics, pain relievers, even antidepressants."

"Your point?"

"Dr. Benton probably kept them somewhere safe.

You said he was old. If he thought someone might break in and steal the goods, he wouldn't keep them in here."

Brianna paused. "We've searched the whole vet space. If they aren't here, where could they be?"

Tracy pressed her lips together. "This can't be all there is; we haven't found the source of the smell."

She used her flashlight to scour the room, stopping on a door with a metal bracket bolted to the wall and a padlock dangling from a hook. "What about that?"

"It goes into his house, I think."

"Then so do we." Tracy walked up and gave the lock a tug. Without bolt cutters, she wasn't getting it open. She cupped her hands around her mouth and shouted at the wood. "Hello? Is anyone in there?"

No response.

She whacked on the upper panel of the door. It echoed. "I don't think it's solid."

"Are you serious?" Brianna joined her and gave the middle panel a solid rap with her knuckles. She laughed. "A massive padlock and a hollow-core door. Who'd have thought?"

"I think that's the idea."

Tracy took a deep breath and kicked a lower panel. It cracked. She did it again and the wood splintered. With a few more well-placed stomps, she broke through enough of the thin wood to squeeze through.

Ducking into the jagged opening, she inhaled and immediately gagged. Bile rose up her throat and saliva pooled in the pockets of her mouth. The smell had grown from nauseating to almost unbearable.

Brianna clambered through behind her and cursed. "I'm gonna hurl. There's got to be a horse dead in here."

"Look for a small medical fridge or a locking cabinet. The good stuff has to be in here somewhere."

Brianna headed toward a hallway and presumably bedrooms and bathrooms, and Tracy took off in the opposite direction, fighting the urge to vomit and run. The house could have been a time capsule of 1955, full of furniture city dwellers paid a fortune to reproduce before the EMP.

A dining room table with angled legs and a rounded top. A three-tier planter on wire legs. A banquette with sliding doors. She pushed one open. Linens and dishes. No medicine.

She eased into the kitchen. White cabinets, Formica countertops with metal edges. Same linoleum floor as the vet side of the house. Tracy opened the cabinets one by one, searching past glassware and pots and pans. Where was the medicine?

Tracy glanced up at the kitchen window. Darkness blanketed the snow and turned their flashlights into homing beacons. The longer the search took, the more dangerous their position became. If someone spotted them, they had nowhere to run.

As Tracy hurried to pull open drawers and eliminate the kitchen, Brianna called out. "Over here!"

Tracy rushed toward the younger woman's voice, gun ready. Her flashlight beam bobbed and weaved down a hallway and into a home office. Brianna stood on the other side of a dark wood desk, bare hand pinching her nose.

"I found the smell. It's not a horse."

Tracy eased around the desk. Brianna's flashlight beam lit up the desiccated form of a man. His skin flaked like bits of paper. His eye sockets sunk into his head like moldy prunes. A syringe lay on the floor beside his shriveled hand.

"I guess Dr. Benton didn't want to tough it out." Brianna eased past the body and tugged open a cabinet.

Tracy's heart fluttered.

CHAPTER FIFTEEN

COLT

Unidentified Farm
  Near Truckee, CA
  4:30 p.m.

"I say we blow it all up like in Eugene." Dani sat on a cleared spot of ground, sheltering Lottie from the cold.

Larkin shook his head. "And lose the potential? No way. It's a working farm. It might have animals, seeds, a bunch of food stored. If we go in there and light it up, we'll lose all that."

"Larkin's right. We need to conserve and focus on getting Walter out with the least amount of damage. Who knows, maybe at some point we can launch an attack and take it over."

"Or they could chase us down and kill everyone."

"I love your optimism."

Dani stuck her tongue out and Colt laughed. "They've got grain silos, Dani. They could be full of enough grain to feed an entire town."

"Then we should do it now. Take everyone out and claim it."

"We don't have the bodies." Larkin stood beside an open door to the Jeep, inventorying their weapons. "With only three of us, we have a good chance to get Walter out, but that's all. Focus on what we can do, not what we want to do later."

Dani turned a lighter over in her hands. "If we can't burn them out, how about smoke?"

Colt perked up. "What do you have in mind?"

"We could draw them out with the threat of fire. Then at least we could scout the place out and see what's there. We might get a handle on their numbers, too."

Larkin nodded. "I like the sound of that. There's plenty of wet wood around here. If we can get some lit, there will be tons of smoke. Set it up on the edge of the farm and they'll have to put it out."

Dani flicked the lighter on and watched the flame. "While they're busy, we swoop in."

Colt thought it over. "Not a bad plan, but what do we do with her?" He motioned to Lottie.

"We can fill up the hot water bottle and build her a sleeping bag nest like last time." Dani lifted her thumb and set the lighter on the Jeep's bumper. "But we need to leave a window open." She glanced at Colt. "In case we don't come back."

"Agreed." Larkin pulled out the readied weapons one by one: three rifles, six backup handguns, spare magazines. He set them all on the tailgate and shut the driver's door. "We can lower this window and muffle some of the cold with a fabric drape. She'll be able to get out if she has to, but the water bottle should keep her warm overnight."

They talked over the strategy of how to approach and where to go first and a backup plan in case something went wrong. After everyone agreed on the best course of action, they broke up.

Larkin and Colt set to harvesting wood. Thanks to a kit they kept in the Jeep at all times, they had everything they needed. Taking turns with a shovel, the men dug out enough fallen branches to burn for hours and laid them on a tarp. Using paracord and a multi-tool, Colt fashioned a set of pull-lines and gave them a tug.

It would be hard work dragging the load down the mountainside and into position. He glanced in the direction of the farm. They had retreated to a spot completely invisible from the valley for safety's sake. While it meant ease of planning, it left them a long road of rocks and close-knit trees to navigate.

The closer they came to the farm, the more exposed they would be. Darkness would be critical. With the tree canopy and slow, fluid movements, they might stay concealed. It was a gamble, but what other choice did they have.

Colt wedged a dry and brittle branch he found

lodged in a tree beneath the wetter limbs. "Dani can light this one. It'll burn while the others smoke."

Larkin nodded. "Let's use some of our supplies, too. The beeswax tinder should stay burning for a while."

Colt left Larkin to finish up and found Dani prepping a space for Lottie in the back seat. With two sleeping bags and a hot-to-the-touch water bottle, she had rigged up a cozy nest. Colt smiled at her handiwork. It would have to do. With any luck, four people would be coming back to the small dog in not too long. He refused to think about her future if they never made it home.

When everything was ready, he crouched in the snow-covered leaves and went over the plan. Colt and Larkin would pull the wood into position. Dani would light it up. Then each person was on their own, heading into the farm and convening at the barn door.

Larkin rose up and held out a bag of jerky and dehydrated fruit leather. "Let's eat. Once it's dark, we'll head in."

It didn't take long. As soon as dusk darkened into the calm of early night, Colt and Larkin hoisted the pulls over their chests. Pull, break, pull. It was agonizing work and sweat broke out across Colt's forehead. He paused halfway down.

"You all right?" Larkin wheezed as he gulped down the frigid night air.

"I'm not getting any younger."

"Tell me about it."

After a moment, they resumed the trek, catching up

to a waiting Dani. She stood behind a tree in a leveled-off area of the mountainside, close enough to the front fence of the farm to make Colt nervous. It was as good a location as any.

"Let's drop it here."

Heaving in time with Larkin, they hoisted the wood into position. Dani rolled the tarp into a log shape and stashed it a hundred yards away. The two men sucked down some water and tossed the empty container into the bushes to hide it from view.

"Ready?" Colt wiped at the sweat on his forehead.

Larkin nodded.

Dani pulled out the lighter. "I'll count to two hundred and light the logs."

"Good." Colt wrapped Dani up in a quick hug before taking her by the shoulders. "Only shoot if you're shot at. Otherwise, stoke the fire and sneak away when they get near."

"Will do."

Colt and Larkin took off, heading closer to the farm with guns drawn and ready. Once they cleared Dani's earshot, Larkin whispered. "You really think this will work?"

"The smoke?"

Larkin nodded.

"It's better than the alternative. If we can draw some of their guards out, we have a chance of grabbing Walter without anyone getting hurt."

"And if we can't?"

"Then we protect ourselves." Colt fell silent. As they neared the fence line of the farm, the first wisps of smoke tickled his nose. "It's showtime." He patted Larkin on the arm. "Good luck."

"Same to you. See you at the Jeep." Larkin took off, disappearing into the night, and Colt did the same.

He eased around the fencing, keeping to the shadows as best he could. The white farmhouse rose in front of him and Colt slowed.

In the closest window, candlelight illuminated a kitchen with a long island. A row of little heads sat with their backs to Colt, all focused on plates in front of them. *Children*. They ranged in size from no bigger than a toddler to elementary school, but all were small and significantly younger than Dani.

Somehow the idea of the farm housing a family had escaped Colt's mind. It had been so long since he'd seen kids, he almost forgot they existed. He glanced behind him. Larger plumes of smoke rose against the forest wall. He had half a mind to rush back to Dani and call it off. They couldn't hurt any kids.

As he struggled with the decision, the door to the main house opened and a man stepped onto the front porch. He flicked on a light and shone it in the direction of the smoke. Colt watched the man's demeanor. First a lean in, then a pan of the light, followed by a panicked, full circle, spin around.

He rushed back inside and in moments, a gaggle of four men tore out the door, each one struggling into a jacket while holding a long gun. Colt sent up a prayer for

Dani to stay hidden. She was an expert at evading detection in a city, but out in the woods was a whole different situation. He hoped she would heed his warning and run.

With four of the farm's residents occupied, Colt crept past the house and on toward the barn.

CHAPTER SIXTEEN

TRACY

Woodland Veterinary Services
  Truckee, CA
  6:00 p.m.

"It has to be in here. At least one." Tracy held out a bag and Brianna dumped everything she could identify by name inside. Fish Mox, painkillers, tranquilizers. So far, nothing for rabies.

"There's got to be something." Tracy willed a vaccine into existence with every twitch of her fingers and beat of her heart. They couldn't have come all this way to leave empty-handed. Visions of Madison growing delirious and combative before succumbing to the virus filled her mind. She twisted the bag in her fingers. "Maybe he kept the vaccines in another place."

Brianna pulled out a white and green box and squinted to read the label. "Shine the light this way."

Tracy sent up a silent prayer. *Please be what we need. Please.*

Brianna tore into the packaging, pulling out a plastic rectangle and folded-up instructions. Her shoulders fell. "It's only a testing kit."

Tracy brightened. A testing kit was better than nothing. "Will it work on the spit we collected?"

"It should." Brianna unfolded the instructions. "We put the saliva on the open spot of the collection tablet and wait ten minutes. A control line should appear in the testing window. If the saliva tests positive, a second red line should appear."

"Just like a pregnancy test." Tracy pulled the jar of saliva they collected from the fox out of her bag. "Are there any gloves around?"

"I saw some back in the office." Brianna hurried into the main veterinary space while Tracy stood beside the mummified Dr. Benton and stared at the test kit. If the saliva came up negative, they could take their time loading up everything useful, find a place to sleep, and head back home in the morning.

If it tested positive...

"Got some." Brianna interrupted Tracy's runaway train of thoughts. "And some Q-tips. Hand me the test."

Tracy held it out and Brianna set it up on the edge of the desk. With gloved hands, she opened the jar. Using the oversized Q-tip, she drew up some of the sample and deposited it on the test. "Now we wait."

Tracy lasted about thirty seconds before the stress of not knowing propelled her into action. She dumped the rest of the medicine into the bag and secured it to her small pack along with the box of gloves Brianna pilfered.

She glanced at her watch. Ten minutes seemed like ten years.

Standing in the dark, with a dead man decaying on the floor, the reality of the world hit Tracy with renewed force. Before the solar storm and the EMP, a ten-minute wait passed in a blur of scrolling. Phones might as well be surgically attached to every person standing in line, waiting in carpool, ordering fast food.

She never noticed how much she relied on a phone to pass the time until they stopped working. Tracy picked up her flashlight and lit up the office, pausing on Dr. Benton's diplomas and photographs hung on the wall. Most chronicled the life of a boy with a crooked smile and a dimple on his left cheek.

On the bookcase, he toddled between two sheep in a field. On the desk, he smiled in front of a school bus with poppy hair falling in his eyes. Prom in the next picture, goodbye at college in the next. The wall held photos commemorating graduation, a first car, and then a wedding.

A handsome young man standing tall beside a lovely bride.

Where is he now? Tracy focused on the syringe on the floor. Did the son know his father took his own life in his office all alone? Did he try to save his old man or write him off as a casualty of the apocalypse? Was he even still alive?

"You ready?"

Tracy snapped back to the present and turned to Brianna. She nodded.

Together, they bent over the test on the edge of the desk. Brianna pointed her flashlight beam at the testing window. One dark bar under C for control. One bright red bar under T for test.

Tracy's spit turned to ash and her tongue to charcoal. "Is that—"

"Positive?" The instructions shook in Brianna's hand. "According to this, it is."

Tracy closed her eyes. The world spun off-kilter.

The fox had rabies. Madison could have rabies. If they didn't find a vaccine, and soon, Tracy's daughter would die a terrible death.

"He has to have a vaccine. It's got to be somewhere." Brianna slid the test and the supplies into a plastic bag and twisted it shut before taking off her gloves. "We just have to look harder." She hurried back to the medicine cabinet, searching through the bottles they already inspected.

Tracy headed back out into the veterinary clinic. Maybe they overlooked a fridge or a hidden drawer. She searched under and over and in and out, turning tables upside down and spilling every jar on the floor.

But it was no use. The vet didn't have a vaccine.

She leaned against the wall, panting and out of breath.

Brianna climbed through the broken door and stood up. "He doesn't have one."

Tracy voiced the words on repeat in her head. "Madison's going to die."

"Not yet." Brianna closed the distance between them, her eyes bright in the flashlight beam. "Some people have lived for months before showing symptoms. We just have to keep searching. If we can find a vaccine and get it to her, she has a good chance."

Tracy palmed her forehead. "Where are we going to find a vaccine now?"

"The hospital. It's our only choice."

"It'll be a war zone."

"Not in the middle of winter."

Tracy shook her head. "It had to be ransacked months ago. There won't be anything left."

"We won't know if we don't try."

"It'll take hours to get there." Tracy fought to keep the despair out of her voice, but she couldn't hold it back. The hospital was too far and too dangerous. "Even if we get there, it'll take days to get home."

"Not necessarily." Brianna held up a set of keys on a Ford keychain. "I found them by the back door. If we can dig out the car, we might have a ride."

Tracy forced her feet to follow Brianna out to the hunk of frozen snow that used to be a car. "We're never going to be able to dig that out."

"Don't say never. Help me find a shovel."

Brianna huffed over to a small shed twenty yards away and Tracy followed, her eyelashes crusting with frozen tears. Snow wedged against the shed door, but with Tracy pulling and Brianna pushing, they managed to open it wide enough for Brianna to slip inside. She whooped as her flashlight lit up the space. "Forget a shovel, we'll melt it out."

Tracy wedged herself in the opening. "What are you—"

Brianna held up a red gas can and baseball bat. "There were some towels in the vet's office. A big stack on top of the cabinets."

"I remember."

"We can wrap them around the bat and use it like a torch. We'll melt the snow in no time."

No time turned out to be an hour, but with some perseverance and an armful of stinky towels, the women melted the majority of the snow and ice. A pale blue Ford Explorer greeted them for their efforts.

"Let's hope it's got enough battery left to crank." Brianna unlocked the driver's-side door and clambered inside.

As Tracy climbed up into the passenger seat, Brianna turned the key. The engine sputtered. Tracy wedged a set of crossed fingers between her pants and the worn velour seat.

On the third pump of gas, the SUV grumbled to life. Tracy's eyes filled with tears. They might be able to save her daughter after all. She cleared her throat. "Are you sure you want to drive?"

Brianna shifted into four-wheel drive and flicked on the headlights. "Definitely. I'm too amped up to sit still. It gives me something to concentrate on." She checked the gauges and hit the steering wheel in triumph. "There's enough gas to get us to the hospital and back home."

"Then let's not waste any time." Tracy buckled her seatbelt and stared out the windshield at the barren landscape lit up in front of them. There was zero chance the hospital wasn't ransacked, but if they were lucky, the vaccines had been ignored. Vandals hit the high-value targets first: oxy and morphine and all the other drugs that took pain away. Then it would be first aid supplies and antibiotics and life-saving medicines for people with chronic illnesses.

Who wanted vaccine in the apocalypse? Tracy hoped it wasn't the first wave of thieves. It was the only chance they had to save her daughter.

Brianna reached out and squeezed her hand. "We'll save Madison."

Tracy nodded. Brianna wasn't giving up and neither should she. If other people lived for months without symptoms and were still cured, then Madison could be, too.

Tracy just had to have faith. She would find a vaccine. She would cure her daughter. Madison wasn't going to survive the insanity after the EMP only to die thanks to a fox bite.

The Explorer bumped over the exit to the farm and onto the road. Thanks to the lingering snow and the lack of vehicular traffic, every road would be an obstacle. It wouldn't be smooth going at top speeds, but a vehicle beat hiking hands down.

Tracy dug into her bag and pulled out a packet of venison jerky and a bottle of water. She handed a bit to Brianna before biting into a strip herself. How their lives had changed in a matter of months.

Gone were snack bars and dollar menus and chocolate croissants from the coffee shop down the street. In their place were dehydrated fruit and veggies and every kind of jerky imaginable. If it could be pickled or jellied or turned into leather, Tracy had learned how.

She'd lost ten pounds of fat and gained that much in muscle. The end of modern civilization had forced her into the best shape of her life. But none of it would matter if she couldn't save Madison. If Walter came home to a dying daughter, Tracy would never forgive herself.

She turned to Brianna. "Thank you for not giving up on us."

Brianna glanced her way with a frown. "Why would I?"

"You helped Madison find her way home when you could have come straight up here to your parents' place. You fought for all of us when the compound came under attack." Tracy swallowed. "When Tucker died, it would have been easy to turn your back and leave us all behind, but you didn't. We'll never be able to thank you enough for all that you and your family have done for us."

"Don't thank me until we find a vaccine."

Tracy shook her head. She meant the words from the bottom of her heart. No matter what happened next— even if she lost her husband and her daughter—Brianna deserved unparalleled praise.

She opened her mouth to say so when the SUV slowed. Tracy leaned forward in her seat. "What is that?"

The younger woman squinted into the dark before turning to Tracy. "I think it's a roadblock."

CHAPTER SEVENTEEN

TRACY

State Route 918
  Truckee, CA
  8:00 p.m.

Brianna took her foot off the gas and Tracy leaned forward, gripping the cracked dash of the borrowed SUV. "Is it a car wreck?"

"I don't think so."

As they eased closer, Tracy's unease grew. It pricked the back of her neck and rose the hair on her arms. Something was wrong. Her voice warbled as she spoke. "Don't stop."

"There's nowhere to go." Brianna swiveled around in the driver's seat. "The last cross street is way behind us."

The headlights illuminated a snowed-over formation spanning both lanes of the road. Too straight to be accidental and too tall to drive over. She fumbled for her flashlight and shined it outside the passenger window. Trees hugged the asphalt, bunched in groups too tight to squeeze through. In the daylight, they might have a chance, but not now with clouds covering the moon and forest blocking their lines of sight.

She clicked off her light. "How far are we from the hospital?"

"A few miles at least. The outskirts of town should be just ahead."

Tracy chastised herself for being complacent. Instead of keeping her eyes and ears open, she'd focused on the hospital and ignored the drive. But she knew better. The woods could always hide a threat.

She glanced at Brianna. Her knuckles matched the snow. "We should turn around and find another way."

The younger woman put the Explorer in reverse. Headlights lit up their rear window. Tracy twisted around, panic rising like acid in her throat. "The vehicle is large, oversized. The headlights are far off the ground." She reached for her rifle. "This isn't just a roadblock."

Brianna spun the wheel. "Make sure your seatbelt's fastened. This could get rough."

Tracy checked the buckle. "How do we want to play this?"

"Like we've been ambushed." Brianna slammed on the brakes as the Explorer finished the turn and jammed it into drive. "They follow us, you start shooting."

Tracy checked the rifle to ensure it was ready to fire. "Will do."

Brianna wasted no time. She pressed the gas pedal to the floor and the SUV fishtailed before accelerating.

The headlights in front of them stayed steady, growing larger and larger as they approached. Tracy ground her teeth together. It was impossible to judge the distance in the dark.

As they neared, the beams of light focused into twin points with the vague shape of a pickup truck beyond. Could a rusty SUV that hadn't been driven in months outrun the truck in front of them?

Tracy wasn't sure. She cranked down the window. "Pass them on the left. I want to get a look."

Brianna nodded. Tracy braced herself. *Closer, closer, closer.*

Cut to black.

The headlights disappeared.

Brianna cursed. "What do I do?"

"Keep going."

Within seconds, they blew past a hulking shape. The pickup hadn't moved. Tracy unbuckled her seatbelt and clambered over the center console.

"What are you doing?"

"They aren't going to let us go." She fell into the back seat as Brianna punched the gas. "Just warn me before you jump a ditch."

Blood pounded in Tracy's skull and her fingers shook on the rifle, but she couldn't let her nerves get the better of her. First Walter, then Madison, now this.

She'd been so deluded into thinking the worst was behind them. Just because they found a safe place to sleep at night didn't mean it was over. The world around them waited to tear their family apart.

Tracy refused to let that happen. Whoever was in that pickup wasn't going to run them off the road or chase them down or even get within five feet of their vehicle.

No way. She would keep them back and they would make it to the hospital. Madison's life depended on it. Her daughter wasn't going to die a painful, agonizing death because Tracy failed.

With a deep breath, she hooked one leg over the rear seat and straddled the back as the SUV bounced down the road. She couldn't gauge speed in the dark, but the slipping wheels and the curses from Brianna up front gave Tracy a pretty good idea. They were going faster than they should on a road covered in snow and ice.

She fell into the cargo area with her pack and her rifle, crunching onto a cardboard box full of something soft and scratchy. She reached inside. *Wool blankets*. Tracy grabbed them by the handfuls, holding her breath as clouds of dust flew in her face. She tossed them on the floor in front of the rear door.

As she kneeled on the blankets, she reached for the glass, running her hands along the edge. *Come on*. She hollered toward the front. "Can you pop the glass from up there?"

Brianna glanced up in the rearview. "Are you crazy? You'll fall out!"

"Do you want me to stop these people or not?"

"We can outrun them."

"What if we can't?" Tracy braced herself with her knees tight against the bottom of the door. "Pop the glass."

Brianna fumbled with buttons on the top of the dash and the lock on the window unlatched. Tracy pushed it open. The wind picked up her hair and blew it across her face. Cold didn't begin to describe it. She sucked back an instant stream of snot and clamped her jaw shut.

I can do this.

Secure against the window, she reached into her bag for a flashlight and her DIY roll of duct tape.

"Any sign of them?"

Tracy glanced up. "We're going too fast. I can't tell if they're back there or if we've lost them." She unrolled a strip of tape. "Give me a minute. I've got an idea."

Brianna kept driving as fast as she could and still keeping control while Tracy wrapped strips of tape around the barrel of the rifle and the light. Once the flashlight was secure, she leaned over and rested the rifle on the rubber window gasket. It wasn't perfect, but thanks to the beat-up cardboard box, she could keep the gun steady.

She shouted at Brianna. "Ready?"

"For anything!"

One benefit of tactical flashlights was the range. Tracy clicked on the light. A clear circle of steady light illuminated the road behind the Explorer and a massive Chevy pickup truck no more than twenty feet behind them.

Tracy shrieked. "They're right behind us! Two men in the front seat!"

"Take them out!"

Tracy took aim. Snow and ice from the Explorer's rear tires flicked into her face. The truck chasing them slammed on its brakes.

No! She pointed at the diminishing shape of the man behind the wheel and fired. The truck shimmied as it came to a stop, receding into the distance as Brianna kept driving.

"Did you hit it?"

"I don't know! They stopped."

The SUV slowed.

"Don't slow down! If I hit it, maybe we can get away!"

Brianna punched the gas and Tracy fell to the side, bringing the rifle with her. The flashlight slammed against the rear door as Tracy's head cracked against the side window. The light flicked out.

"You okay?"

Tracy palmed her head with a wince, checking for a wound. *No blood.* She exhaled in relief. "Yeah." As she picked herself up, she reached for the flashlight. "Keep driving."

Please be gone. Please, please be gone. Tracy repositioned herself on the blankets and propped the gun back on the window before reaching for the flashlight. She clicked it back on.

The wind ripped her scream away. A huge grille bore down on the SUV and Tracy fought to keep a handle on her wits and the rifle. She leaned down to aim when the truck's headlights flashed on bright. All she could see was light.

She blinked and spots swam in her vision. *Damn it!*

Brianna shouted from the front. "Get down!"

Tracy pulled the rifle off the back and fell onto the floor. "I can't see."

"They're gaining."

Tracy blinked. Flashes of red and white bounced in front of her eyes. She fumbled for the seat back.

"I think they're gonna ram us!" Brianna half-shrieked. "I can't go any faster!"

They couldn't get run off the road. If the truck hit them, Brianna would lose control. Tracy blinked again and the red blended into spotty shapes. She couldn't climb up into the front and wait for the people in the truck to take them out.

She had to fight back. *No giving up. No admitting defeat.* Tracy grunted as she shoved the cardboard box toward the back.

"What are you doing?"

"Ending this." Tracy inhaled through her nose and pulled the rifle up onto the box. It cleared the window ledge by an inch. Thanks to the high beams, she couldn't see, but it didn't matter.

She had a full magazine and an extra after that. If she didn't hit the driver after thirty rounds, then she might as well let them kill her. She exhaled and took aim two feet above the center of the right light.

Pull, pull, pull. Tracy fired off shot after shot, not

stopping until the entire magazine was empty. The truck rattled and shook. The horn blared.

She held her breath. The headlights began to fade and bounce. As she watched, they wobbled to the left and veered off the road.

"Did you hit them?"

Tracy waited to make sure. "I think so. It looks like it's in the ditch."

Brianna whooped for joy. "Way to go!"

Tracy reached out with shaky fingers for the open window and pulled it down via the latch. She managed to shut it after a few tries with a solid yank that sent her flying.

The truck's headlights faded and the back of the SUV darkened.

I did it. I really did it.

Tracy stayed on her back, catching her breath until the last of the light from the pickup truck disappeared. Only then did she climb back over the seat and the console and join Brianna in the front.

Her daughter's best friend reached out and grabbed her hand. "Thank you, Tracy."

"Thank *you*. That was some fine driving." She reached down to the floor and fished out a bottle of water. After draining half of it, she handed it to Brianna, who finished it off. "Do you think you can still find the hospital?"

Brianna nodded. "We can come at it from the east. It's a bit longer route, but assuming we don't hit any more roadblocks, we should be there within the hour."

Tracy buckled her seatbelt and leaned back. Hopefully by the time they found the hospital, she could catch her breath.

CHAPTER EIGHTEEN

COLT

Unidentified Farm
   Near Truckee, CA
   8:00 p.m.

The barn door loomed ahead. Colt hugged the worn
siding, keeping low and out of sight. So far, he'd
encountered zero resistance. Either a million men waited
inside the barn, or the operation was significantly smaller
than it appeared.

He stopped at the corner. With a rifle slung over his
shoulder, his Sig in his hand, and a backup Glock 19 in
an appendix holster, he had enough firepower to handle a
small platoon. But the sight of the children nagged him.
Dani had been practically an orphan and when he found
her; it wasn't pretty.

Killing a father didn't sit well with him. Colt exhaled.
He would only shoot if absolutely necessary.

Using his free hand, he slid the door to the barn open enough to squeeze through. It wasn't a stable. The entire place had been turned into living quarters. He slid the door shut and faced a small antechamber.

Walls had been roughed-in a ten-by-ten-foot room with a door leading to additional areas beyond. No taller than eight feet in height, the walls lacked paint. Drywall mud tracked across the seams and nail holes.

Someone knew how to build but didn't have the time or money to finish. He frowned. It wasn't what he expected. How many rooms waited on the other side? Colt strode toward the interior door.

He put his ear up to the hollow core. *Silence.*

The handle turned in his grip and he swung the door out wide, gun up and ready. A hallway greeted him.

Shit.

Rooms flanked the hall all the way down the length of the barn, five on each side at least. He would have to search one by one to find Walter. How many were empty? How many held someone who could sound an alarm?

He stepped with caution along the unfinished plywood floor, counting the rooms and assessing the odds. Eleven more closed doors on the sides and one at the end. Based on the ceiling, the hallway ended short, only three-quarters of the way down the length of the barn. He guessed the final door led to a great room. Maybe a cafeteria or a meeting space. A place to house vehicles.

Colt sucked in a breath. It didn't smell like gasoline

or rubber. It smelled like a barn. Rough wood and dirt and stale animal stink.

It hadn't been converted to human space for long.

He hurried back to the beginning and braced himself for door number one across from the antechamber. With a quick turn of the knob, it opened. Colt exhaled. Empty.

A bunk bed flanked the far wall and a pair of small desks perched against the other. A dorm room. Or a barracks. He shut the door and kept going.

The next three were the same. All empty, all made for two people.

He was beginning to think this place was more than a family farm. The next door opened to an office with a single desk, rows of bookshelves stuffed to the gills behind it. He eased inside and scanned the titles.

Archery 101.

Farming for Urbanites.

Field Dressing for Dummies.

Shoot First.

He frowned. Everything someone would need to start over in the new America and stay alive doing it. Urgency mixed with dread in Colt's veins and he wiped a burst of sweat off his forehead.

The next room smelled of wool and mothballs and contained more clothes and blankets and towels than Colt had seen in one place outside of a department store. He shut the door and kept going. More barracks. They could house eighteen people in the barn, two to a room.

Colt swallowed. Eighteen people prepped to fight would be a formidable force. He hoped Dani was following his instructions. She couldn't defend herself against even half that many. She needed to hide.

Stepping back into the hallway, Colt paused. The large room at the end beckoned. If Walter was still in the barn, he had to be there. He readied himself and opened the door.

The first thing that hit him was the smell. Not of horses or manure or a stable full of farm equipment, but coffee. Fresh-brewed coffee.

Four long wood tables occupied the middle of the space with a roughed-in kitchen along the far wall. Comfortable chairs were clumped on the end with coffee tables and stacks of books. It was a rec room. And it wasn't empty.

Walter sat at a table, coffee mug in one hand and a half-eaten biscuit in the other. Colt shut the door and rushed him. "Let's get out of here."

Walter blinked. "Colt? What are you doing here?"

"Rescuing you. Come on."

"What? No, no." Walter shook his head. "You've got it all wrong."

Colt spied the bandage on his shoulder. "You were shot! I knew it." He reached for the other man's arm. "Dani and Larkin are outside. We need to go, now."

"Is that what the commotion is about? Oh, Colt. This will never work."

"Of course it will as long as we hurry."

An oversized exterior door on the other side of the room slid open and a lantern bobbed in the air. A stream of children filed in, one after the other, and took their seats on a bench at one of the tables. Ranging in age from four to at least sixteen, they all stopped and stared when they spotted Colt.

Whispers ran down the length of the table as a woman in black pants and parka entered the room. With hair the color of terra-cotta, she reminded Colt of the flight attendant back in Eugene.

When she saw Colt, she froze. "Can I help you?"

Colt glanced at Walter. "I'm taking this man out of here."

"I'm afraid you'll have to talk to Benjamin about that."

"No, I don't." Colt moved closer to Walter and dropped his voice. "Come with me now and you can explain everything later."

Walter smiled at the woman. "It's okay, Jenny. He won't hurt me."

"You know the rules, Walt. We can't let him leave."

Colt's eyes bounced back and forth. *Jenny? Walt?* Did they know each other? What the hell was going on?

A shout rose from outside the barn and Colt's insides twisted. He would recognize that voice anywhere.

"Stay still!" A man's booming voice cut off the scream.

"Ben!" Jenny cupped her mouth and shouted at the open doorway. "In here!"

A moment later, one of the men Colt watched rush from the house entered dragging Dani along behind. She looked around in a panic, blood dripping from a wound in her scalp. It coated her cheek and fell to the floor in fat, wet plops.

"Dani!"

She jerked her head toward Colt's voice and the man holding her brought up his gun: a shotgun with a short barrel and a pistol grip. Based on the way he held it, Colt guessed he could fire it one-handed without a problem and put a hole half a foot wide in Colt's chest.

Not good.

"Who the hell are you?"

Jenny volunteered. "He says he's here to take Walt."

"Like hell he is." Ben's grip twisted in Dani's hair and the girl lashed out, pelting his shin with kicks.

"Let me go, you overgrown troll!"

The man laughed. "For someone who tried to burn down my farm, you're not much of a fighter."

"We didn't try to burn it down. We created a distraction." Colt took a step forward. "Let her go."

"Or what?"

Colt frowned at the children. All seven of them huddled together, the oldest clutching the arm of the littlest as she cried. He didn't want to shoot anyone. He didn't want to harm the kids or leave them orphans.

"I don't want to hurt your family."

"You won't." Ben turned and shouted into the dark. "Harris, Killian, get in here!"

In moments, two more men appeared, each one armed.

"Daddy!" One of the little girls, no older than five or

six, hopped off the bench, but the closest man stuck out his arm.

"Not now, baby."

The girl stopped, a sob bubbling up her throat.

Colt's frown deepened. He could make it out of there, but only if he shot the place to hell.

This wasn't like Eugene where he didn't care if Jarvis or his men survived. He wasn't a child-killer. He wasn't a widow-maker.

He swallowed and set his handgun on the table before holding up his hands.

Ben nodded. "Rifle, too."

Colt unslung the rifle before setting it next to the Sig. "I've got a Glock in my belt."

"Then get rid of it."

Colt pulled the gun from the holster and added it to the pile.

"What are you doing? Why aren't you fighting back?" Dani twisted in her captor's grip, but Colt merely exhaled.

"We're outnumbered."

"So what!" She tried to kick Ben again and he cursed beneath his breath. The other two men approached and he let them take Dani. She fought the whole time until they pinned her arms behind her back.

Unencumbered, Ben rolled his neck. "You all right, Walter?"

"I'm fine."

"Do you know these people?"

"I do." Walter glanced at Colt with an unreadable expression. "But I didn't ask them to come."

"Is this how your group acts? They rush in, ready to take what isn't theirs?"

"They thought I was in trouble. They're here to rescue me."

Ben turned to Colt. "Is that true?"

"It is."

"You've done a piss-poor job of it if you ask me."

The oldest kid on the bench snickered and Ben pinned him with a look. "Help everyone go back to bed, will you, Sam? The emergency is over."

"Oh, Uncle Ben, come on. It's early."

"It's past your bedtime, Taylor, and you know it."

Colt watched as the woman walked up to Ben and whispered in his ear. He glanced at Colt and nodded.

One by one the kids filed out of the barn and Jenny followed. Her voice carried back inside. "Hurry up everyone. It's cold and you aren't properly dressed."

As the last sounds of the kids faded, Ben's face hardened. He turned to the other two men. "Take them all to the stables. They can sleep there tonight."

CHAPTER NINETEEN

TRACY

Mountain Valley Hospital
    Truckee, CA
    10:00 p.m.

A gray concrete building loomed ahead, white and red emergency signs broken and dark. Brianna killed the headlights at the first sign and eased over to the side of the road.

She turned to Tracy. "How do we want to do this?"

"Let's stash the vehicle and come at it on foot."

Brianna nodded and navigated behind an abandoned strip mall that used to house a sporting goods store and a karate school. "I don't have a clue where a vaccine might be."

Tracy frowned. "Neither do I. Most likely spots are the pharmacy and the ER."

"Both of which are going to be trashed."

"Then we do the best we can. If we're lucky, no one took the vaccines." Tracy tightened her bag on her back and checked the second rifle magazine. She knew what a long shot the hospital would be, but they didn't have a choice. Madison had to have the vaccine. Tracy refused to think about the alternative.

They shut and locked the SUV and together headed toward the hospital. Keeping to the shadows, it didn't take long. Tracy's nose wrinkled as they entered the parking lot.

"Ugh. What's that smell?"

"Do you really want to know?" Visions of an overflowing morgue filled Tracy's mind. "How long could the place keep running on backup generators?"

"A few days."

"After that, everyone in intensive care died."

"And a whole host of other people, too." Brianna pointed at the front doors to the ER. Even in the moonlight, Tracy could make out the giant circle with a slash mark through it. As they neared, a scrawled out CLOSED came into view.

"Didn't seem to stop people."

Every window on the first floor that didn't have plywood nailed to it was broken.

Brianna shuddered against a gust of wind. "How long do you think it's been like this?"

"Months." Tracy picked her way through frozen bits of trash in the parking lot. Thanks to the sheer number of abandoned cars, the snow hadn't piled up more than an inch or two.

Together, the women snaked their way up to the front. With temperatures falling into the teens, no one was foolish enough to be outside, but that didn't mean the hospital would be empty.

Tracy reached for Brianna's arm as they got to the broken windows of the emergency room. "There's liable to be all sorts of people living inside. We need to be careful."

Brianna nodded. "Let's search the ER first. Then we'll find the pharmacy."

Tracy stepped over the broken glass and into the hospital. Snowdrifts piled in the corners. Wadded-up paper and plastic and crushed bottles littered the floor. She clicked on her flashlight and Brianna did the same.

"Whoa." Brianna panned the lobby with a slow arc of light. "It's straight out of a disaster movie."

She was right. They had been inside ransacked stores and survived the chaos of Chico State, but Tracy had never seen anything like the Truckee hospital. If it wasn't nailed down, it was smashed, ripped, or mangled.

Holes gaped like hungry mouths in the walls. Springs stuck through the torn fabric of a sagging couch. Soot tracked across the ceiling. A trash can sat in the corner, nestled among scorched and broken bits of wood. Squatters, keeping themselves warm.

Tracy slung the rifle across her body and reached for the Glock. She needed freedom of movement. "Let's head to the nurses' station. There has to be a directory."

Brianna hopped the counter. "Watch your step. It's a

mess." She eased forward and Tracy followed a few paces behind.

She found a map on the wall beside a pair of double doors. "Here."

According to the map, a central dispensary for the ER was in the southwestern corner. Tracy took off, half running down the hall. She knew before she reached the counter that it would be hopeless.

Every step brought more destruction. Graffiti on the walls, doors off their hinges. Dried blood pooled on the floor.

Tracy shuddered.

"Don't give up. We'll find it." Brianna squeezed Tracy's arm as she eased past to take the lead. She stopped in front of the counter and grimaced. Where sliding glass windows used to be, only broken shards remained. She tried to smile. "At least it's easier to get inside."

Both women scrambled over the counter and found themselves in a war zone. Boxes and bottles and used syringes littered the floor. Shelves were broken and leaning against each other. Cabinet doors lay in front of empty shelves.

"There's nothing left."

Brianna shrugged off the doom. "Let's check to make sure."

An hour later, even Brianna's optimism faded. She slumped against the only standing shelving unit and wiped at the sweat dripping off her nose. "We need to find a map. The main hospital pharmacy should be on this floor."

Tracy stripped off her sweater and tied it around her waist before tugging her hair up into a haphazard bun. "If the ER didn't have a single usable Band-Aid, the pharmacy won't have a vaccine."

Brianna pushed herself upright. "We won't know unless we look for ourselves."

Tracy knew Brianna was right, but she couldn't help but voice the despair threatening to drag her under. It swelled inside her belly, a thick black sludge of horror. Her daughter was going to die—not after living a long and happy life, with a husband and kids and a house of her own, but in the middle of nowhere in the dead of winter.

Alone.

It wasn't the dream Tracy had for her daughter's future. She forced down a wave of nausea. Tracy had spent the last nine months focused on their current predicament, surviving every day as it came. She hadn't stopped to think about the long-term ramifications of their situation.

Gone were spring weddings with bouquets of peonies, lush grass beneath chubby baby feet, front porches where friends stopped to share a pitcher of tea. Somehow, Tracy had held onto a kernel of hope that they could find it all again.

In quiet moments, she'd think, maybe the government would get itself together. Maybe other countries would come in and lend much-needed aid.

She braced herself with an outstretched hand against the wall. No one was coming to push the reset button. They could eke out an existence with Brianna's family, but unless they found another community to join, their little band of ten might as well be the last people left on earth.

Tracy closed her eyes. Eight if Madison and Walter died. She shook her head. Enough wallowing. "Let's find the pharmacy."

Brianna brightened. "I knew you'd come around." She scampered over and wrapped Tracy up in an unexpected hug. The young woman's dirty curls tickled her nose. "We're going to save Madison. You have to have faith."

As Brianna pulled away, Tracy forced her lips to curve into a smile. "You're right."

Think positive thoughts. She repeated the mantra over and over as they climbed over the wreckage and back into the hospital hallway.

Exhaustion tugged at her legs and Tracy checked her watch. Two in the morning already. She smacked her cheeks to focus before picking a direction. "I vote this way. The pharmacy is probably across the hospital and away from the ER."

The two women picked their way through trash and broken glass until they reached a set of double doors. A sign overhead read Orthopedics, Geriatrics, and Pharmacy. Tracy buzzed with hope.

Brianna pushed the doors open and they walked into a calmer side of the hospital. With every step, Tracy's excitement grew. It was almost normal. No trash, no broken glass, no graffiti. It didn't make sense, but she wasn't going to look a gift horse in the mouth. "Maybe this side wasn't hit."

She lit up a map at the corner of a four-way intersection of halls. "The pharmacy is this way." Tracy turned down the western hall and practically broke into a run. She slammed into another pair of double doors, expecting them to swing open. They didn't budge. She hit them again.

"Are they stuck?" Brianna hurried to join in, pushing against the right-side door while Tracy pushed on the left. Not a chance.

Tracy backed up and shone her flashlight all around. No locks, no automatic buttons. It didn't make sense. She stood on her tiptoes and looked through the plexiglass window. The hallway beyond sat empty and deserted.

She lowered back to the ground, confused. "The pharmacy should be twenty feet down the hall. This doesn't make sense."

Brianna crouched in front of the doors and wedged a hunting knife blade between them. The fuzzy felt trim gave way and Brianna's knife slid in an inch. She frowned and pushed harder. "There's something on the other side. It's hard." She jabbed the knife in again. "I can't pierce it."

"Like a cross bar?"

Brianna ran the knife up and down the seam, testing the theory. After a moment, she nodded. "It's about four inches tall and right in the middle of the doors."

Tracy swallowed. "Hospitals don't have security gates in the middle of their hallways."

"Especially not when the pharmacy is on the other side."

"Someone else did this." Tracy turned around. "And they don't want uninvited guests."

"What are we going to do?"

"Find another way in. With it barricaded off, the pharmacy might be untouched." Tracy tamped down her excitement as her brain struggled to keep up with her runaway heart. "Let's backtrack. There's got to be another way in."

The women hurried to the map on the wall. The hallway was the only interior access to that portion of the hospital. Brianna cursed. "We can't break it down without a battering ram."

Tracy thought it over. If they couldn't come at it from this floor, they had three choices: up, down, or all the way around. She turned to Brianna with an idea taking shape in her mind. "What's the number one place no one wants to go in a hospital when the power goes out?"

Brianna shrugged.

"The basement."

"Why?"

Tracy swallowed. "It's the morgue."

DAY 282

CHAPTER TWENTY

TRACY

Location Unknown
Near Truckee, CA
4:00 a.m.

"I thought the smell at the vet was bad." Brianna tied her sweater around her face and leaned into the stink like a head wind. "We're going to have to burn these clothes when we get home."

Tracy followed three steps behind, her flashlight beam bouncing off gurneys piled with bones and desiccated bits of flesh. A skull with hair still attached lay on the floor. A shirt covered a bag of bones slumped in a wheelchair. She swallowed down the horror and kept walking.

Imagining the first frantic days in the hospital after the EMP brought the whole grisly scene to life. Critical-care patients dying. Doctors and nurses fleeing to protect their families. Looters and thieves coming to pillage before the dead were even cold.

Brianna stopped at a door marked Emergency Exit. "Is this it?"

"Must be." Tracy pushed the door open and shined her light inside. The stairs only led up. "Let's go."

The women proceeded with caution up to the first-floor landing. Tracy clicked off her light and plunged the stairwell into darkness. "We should be inside the barricade. Close to the pharmacy. Ready?"

"As I'll ever be." Brianna pushed the door open and waited.

No noise. No light. She stepped out into the hall and Tracy followed, closing the door as quietly as she could.

It was too dark to see anything. She waved her hand in front of her face. *Nothing.* They couldn't stand there for an hour and hope their eyes adjusted. Ripping off her sweater, she fashioned a cover for the flashlight with several layers of wool and clicked it on.

Low, diffuse light illuminated a circle of about four feet. It would have to do.

Tracy took the lead and kept the light trained low. Twenty feet ahead the wall gave way to a door and she lifted the flashlight. PHARMACY stood out in large block letters above a frosted window.

With a deep breath, she tugged the door open. A waiting area sat untouched and orderly on the other side.

"Someone went to a lot of trouble to keep this safe." Brianna pulled out her own flashlight and clicked it on, flooding the room with light.

Neat, tidy shelves full of medicine beckoned them from behind a counter. Tracy pulled the sweater off her flashlight and hurried forward. It didn't seem real.

"We need to be fast. This place has to be watched, even in the winter. If the guards are on rounds, we don't have long."

With a hop of excitement, Tracy scaled the counter and landed on two feet in front of at least twenty rows of shelves. There had to be enough medicine to treat hundreds of people. Hope filled her heart as she rushed toward the closest shelving unit.

The labels read like a library shelf and Tracy almost giggled. She knew how to find her way around an alphabetized storeroom. Vaccines would either be on the end or in a fridge. She called out to Brianna as she ran down the length of the pharmacy. "Find a fridge! The vaccines might be there."

Tracy turned the corner and used the flashlight to read the labels on the final row of shelves. *Tagamet, Tenivac, Thyro-Tabs.* She ran a few feet and kept reading. *Ultiva, Udavex, Varenicline.* No vaccine section.

Damn it. She circled back to the Rs one row over, hoping for more luck, when Brianna called out. "I found the fridge! It's got tons of shots in it."

Tracy rushed toward Brianna's voice. She found her hunched over a short fridge near the phone bank at the front of the pharmacy. As the younger woman rooted through the vials, a bright light lit them up from behind.

Oh, no. Tracy spun around and held her hand up to ward off the glare. She couldn't see anything.

"Identify yourselves." The deep male voice boomed in the quiet space.

Tracy stood her ground. "Who are you?"

"People you don't want to mess with."

The light slid toward the ground and Tracy squinted past it. Two men stood at the pharmacy entrance. One held a floodlight. The other a rifle aimed straight at Brianna's chest. Tracy reached for the girl's hand and squeezed as she whispered. "I'll distract them. First chance you get, run."

Brianna shook her head. "I'm not leaving you or the vaccine."

Tracy stepped forward.

The man with the gun shifted to point at her. "Stop where you are."

"Please, we don't mean any harm." She held up one hand. "We only need a vaccine."

"What for?"

"To cure my daughter."

The man with the light lifted it to shine on Brianna. "She looks fine."

"Not her. My daughter back home. She was bit by a fox infected with rabies."

The flashlight man snorted. "In the middle of winter? Yeah, right."

"I'm serious. It was caught in a trap. She thought it was dead."

The two men shared a few words, voices low and gravelly.

Tracy turned to Brianna. "Have you found it yet?"

"No."

Damn it. She turned back around as the man with the gun spoke up.

"You two tweakers?"

"No."

"You smell like tweakers."

Tracy bit her tongue to keep from cursing. "We walked through the morgue."

The armed man laughed. "Definitely tweakers. No sober person would do that."

"We're not high and we're not strung out. We're desperate. We need a rabies vaccine."

"And I need a wind farm." He pointed with his gun. "Come on, let's go."

"No."

His shoulders rose and fell in obvious frustration. "I'm not going to ask again."

Tracy jerked her head back toward Brianna. "When I shoot, run." As she twisted back around, she brought up the Glock.

"I wouldn't do that if I were you."

"Oh, yeah? Watch me." Tracy aimed at the flashlight and fired. The lens shattered and the room plunged into darkness.

A volley of shots rang out as Tracy dove for the ground. Searing pain lanced her upper arm.

"Tracy! Are you okay?" Brianna scrambled toward her.

More shots rang out. A bullet ricocheted off the floor and whizzed by Tracy's ear.

"Get behind a shelf! They won't shoot into the medicine!"

Tracy crawled into the closest aisle, keeping as low to the ground as she could until she reached the end. She slipped behind the end cap and sucked in a breath. Blood slicked her left arm and dripped off her fingers.

Brianna found her moments later, a flurry in the dark. "Are you okay?"

Tracy tried not to groan. "I might have taken a bullet."

"Oh my God."

"It's not that bad."

"What can I do?"

Tracy eased her bag off her shoulder. "Find the compression bandage."

Brianna rifled through the bag and pulled out a small shrink-wrapped plastic item. She ripped it open. "I'll need a light to see."

Tracy pulled out her flashlight and clicked it on. Blood already soaked her shirt and puddled on the floor. "Do it."

As Brianna slid the bandage around Tracy's arm, she groaned. "Hurry. We're sitting ducks back here."

Wrapping over and over, Brianna covered the absorption pad before twisting the elastic wrap into a cord. She shoved the closure bar under the cord and turned it to tighten the bandage.

Tracy gritted her teeth as Brianna hooked the bar to the bandage and secured it in place. Only then did she click off the light.

"Is that too tight?"

"We'll see if my arm falls off." Tracy fought back a wave of nausea and vertigo. "Thank you."

"Don't thank me yet. We're still trapped."

"There has to be another way out."

"I'll look." Before Tracy could say another word, Brianna rushed off into the dark. It took all of Tracy's self-control to not close her eyes and slip into unconsciousness.

She cradled her arm in her lap and focused on Madison. Her daughter needed her to make it out of there alive and with a vaccine.

A scurry of footsteps sounded and Tracy blinked.

"There's no other way." Brianna slid next to Tracy and took cover behind the shelf. "We're in a cave."

"Then we'll have to fight our way out." Tracy readied the Glock. "At least they hit my nondominant arm."

Brianna checked the shotgun. "Can you shoot?"

"We don't have a choice. You find the vaccine. I'll give you cover."

As Brianna stood up, a metal clang sounded at the front of the pharmacy. Something rolled across the linoleum.

"What is that?"

A tremendous boom shook the entire room and a light blasted impossibly bright. Tracy couldn't hear, couldn't think, couldn't see. Everything spun out of control. *Am I dying? Is this what it feels like?* She tried to stand and ran into something hard. Boxes and bottles rained down from overhead.

She fell to the floor. Her knee slammed into the ground and she rolled over. It wasn't death. It was something worse.

A flashbang.

Tracy remembered her husband describing the device and wishing they had some for defense. Her ears rang and she couldn't see. She was blind and deaf.

"Brianna!" Tracy shouted, unable to hear her own voice.

A hand wrapped around her wounded arm and she screamed into the void.

The grip tightened and the searing pain snapped her back into reality. Her vision returned in splotchy, swirling moments.

A man held her by the arm. He scowled as she blinked.

She opened her mouth to scream again when the barrel of a gun swam in her face.

As a sharp pain crashed into her temple, the blurry world went black.

CHAPTER TWENTY-ONE

COLT

Unidentified Farm
   Near Truckee, CA
   6:00 a.m.

Dani's shouts echoed inside the barn and Colt gritted his teeth to keep from reaching for a weapon. Ben still held the shotgun pointed straight at Colt. About Colt's age, maybe a few years older with the first hints of gray at his temples, the man didn't come across weak or indecisive.

If anything, he was too quick to judge. He motioned for Colt to approach. "You're next."

"I'm not going anywhere until you tell me what's going on."

"You aren't the one in charge here." With a frame straight out of center linebacker position, he probably didn't need to use that line too often, but Colt wasn't scared.

He glanced at Walter. "You're fine with this guy ordering all of us around?"

Walter's jaw ticked. It was the first sign Colt had that the man wasn't one hundred percent on board. "It's not our property."

"Damn straight it isn't." Ben motioned again with the gun. "Now let's move. Walter, you stay here and wait for me to come back."

"Just do what he says. It'll be all right." Walter nodded at Colt. Was that anger in his eyes?

Colt eased past his friend and toward Ben. Now was his best chance.

"Don't even think it." Ben prodded him with the barrel of the shotgun and Colt relented. If he reached for the rifle, he'd be dead before he fired a single shot.

He would have to wait for another opportunity.

As Ben pushed him outside, he caught sight of Dani. A lantern sat a yard or so from her feet and as she scrambled and kicked, she cast shadows across the faded red paint of the closest barn.

One of her escorts fumbled with a door lock while the other tried to hold her. He wasn't having much luck. Colt cheered her on in silence. They might not be able to escape, but she could at least give them a workout.

As Colt approached, Dani slammed her foot down on top of the big man's toes. He yelped and his arms loosened in response to the pain. Dani seized the opportunity. Before Colt could shout to warn her, she lunged for the man's handgun perched in an open-carry holster on his hip.

Her fingers wrapped around the grip and Colt held his breath. In a matter of seconds, it was over. Dani stood, panting for breath, three feet away from her captor, gun pointed straight at his face.

Ben shouted, "Don't be stupid. We've got eyes on you from all over." Colt tensed. Could that be true? Were there others out in the dark, waiting for an opportunity to take them out?

"I wouldn't be so sure about that." Larkin's voice cut through the standoff as he emerged from the tree line. "From what I can tell, it's just us."

Ben poked Colt in the back with the shotgun. "Let me guess. He's with you."

"Bingo."

"Who the hell are you people?"

"Just a tight-knit group who protects their own." Colt sucked in a breath. He couldn't just stand there and do nothing, but a shotgun to the back hampered his efforts. "How about you let us go so we can get out of here?"

"So I'm supposed to believe you'll just walk away?"

"That's exactly what we'll do. You let Walter and the rest of us go and you'll never have to see us again."

Ben was unimpressed. "Right."

Colt was unfettered. "You have my word."

"How do I know you're not lying?"

"You'll have to trust me."

Ben fell silent.

I'm getting through to him. Colt turned enough to catch Ben's eye. "I think what you're doing here is noble.

If we'd met under different circumstances, we might have become allies."

"Walter said the same thing."

"Walter's a good man." Colt almost had him. A little more talking and Ben would come around. He opened his mouth to push harder when an unmistakable sound pierced the air.

A single gunshot.

Colt spun around in time to see Dani hit the ground. "No!" His shout boomed through the farm and Colt took off, running to reach her. Three feet away, something slammed against his right knee and it buckled.

He fell forward, arms outstretched. His chest hit the ground and bits of snow pelted his face. Dani turned her head toward his. Blood tinged the snow around her torso.

She blinked.

Colt rose up. A boot shoved him back down. A gun barrel smashed into his temple.

"You so much as blink and I'll put a hole through your skull."

"You bastards. She didn't do anything to you. She didn't deserve this." Colt stared at Dani.

"I'm sorry, Colt. I tried to stop them." Larkin's voice, laced with pain, called out from the other side of the farm. Colt twisted his head. Larkin stood on the edge of the light, clutching his stomach. A man pointed a rifle straight at his head.

Colt turned back to Dani. Her face paled by the second. He was losing her. After everything they had been through together. After all the struggles, he was going to watch her die in the middle of a stranger's farm. And for what?

No. He wasn't going to let that happen. "Larkin?"

"Yeah?"

"You remember the movie they always played on Friday nights at Reed?"

"Butch Cassidy and the Sundance Kid?"

"How's it end again?" Colt didn't wait for Larkin to answer. Instead he channeled all his strength, all his anger, all the pent-up rage of living for nine months in the apocalypse, and flipped himself over. Ben stumbled back from the force of it and Colt lunged, jumping up like a tiger on the attack. He grabbed for the shotgun as it discharged.

A handful of bird shot ripped holes in his jacket arm, but most of it flew wide. Larkin fought his own war on the other side of the farm, shouting and carrying on. Another gun discharged. Colt didn't have time to look.

He yanked harder on the shotgun, but Ben refused to let go.

Twisting around, the bigger man pressed the gun straight into Colt's heart. "Give me a reason."

Colt opened his mouth to give him plenty when headlights lit up the entire place. A truck roared down the drive and stopped just short of the clearing. Colt scanned the area for Larkin. His friend was on the ground, zip ties around his wrists and ankles.

Damn it.

He turned to Dani. She was still sprawled in the snow, eyes wide, mouth open. *Come on, give me something.* Colt willed her to move. A twitch, a flutter of a finger. *Anything.*

He held his breath. She blinked.

Colt bit back a sob. Dani was still alive. He rose up. "She needs help. She's going to bleed out while you stand there with your thumb up your ass."

Ben pushed him back down with a nudge of the barrel against his shoulder. "Get down or you join her."

Shouts erupted from the other side of the farm. Colt flipped his head over.

"We caught two of them in the hospital." A man fireman-carried a smaller person toward the scene in the snow. He stopped ten feet from Ben. "What the hell?"

"We've had a bit of a disturbance here, too."

"Where should I put her?"

"In the stable. We'll keep them all there overnight."

The man carrying the unconscious woman took off, cutting through the space between Larkin and Colt. A shock of blonde curls flopped against his back as he headed toward the barn. *It can't be.*

Colt twisted back the other way. *Crap.* There was no mistaking that unruly hair. Brianna was one of the women. But who was the other?

The second man followed, carrying a woman with a bandage wrapped around her upper arm. It was soaked in blood. *Oh, no.* Colt couldn't believe it. What were they doing in the hospital?

He had to alert Walter. With a deep breath, Colt began to shout. "Walter! Walter Sloane! Walter!"

Ben kicked him in the side, but he kept shouting. "Walter!"

"Tracy!" Walter's voice rose above the din. "What the hell?" His feet ran past Colt. "Put her down. That's my wife!"

Ben bellowed toward the barn. "Stand down!"

Walter kept running.

A gunshot cracked in the night. "Stop running or I'll shoot him."

Walter slowed, his eyes darting between Colt and Dani on the ground and Tracy still dangling unconscious from the man's shoulder. He shook his head, unable to make sense of it. "That's my wife Daniel's carrying. What happened to her?"

"She was found somewhere she didn't belong."

"Then she had a damn good reason."

"We'll get to the bottom of it. But for now, she goes in the stable."

Walter argued and Colt tuned him out. Dani needed him. He turned back and her eyelids fluttered. *Stay with me, sweetheart. Stay with me.* Colt reached out a hand.

Her lips were blue.

He touched her cheek. Cool and clammy.

She closed her eyes.

No! He couldn't bear it. Forget the kids he'd seen earlier. Forget all the people on the farm he didn't even know. They let the best person he'd ever met suffer while they bickered like children. *No more.*

It didn't matter if Walter thought they could be allies.

It didn't matter if Colt didn't make it out alive. Dani meant more to him than another sunrise.

He would avenge this injustice and she would make it out of there alive. He would take these people straight with him to hell. He dug one knee into the snow and pushed up to stand.

"Christ. Not you again."

Colt turned, ready to take Ben out with all his fury. A crack lit his ear on fire.

He was unconscious before he hit the ground.

CHAPTER TWENTY-TWO

WALTER

Jacobson Family Farmhouse
Near Truckee, CA
7:00 a.m.

Walter stared at the unconscious form of his wife. Her hair dusted the snow as the son of bitch who carried her stomped toward the barn. The scene before him was straight out of some of their worst days after the EMP.

Dani bleeding all over the ground. Colt unconscious beside her. Larkin hog tied and furious. Brianna and Tracy dangling like sacks of potatoes from strangers' shoulders. Walter clenched his fists and fought back a rising swell of rage.

It boiled and thickened in his gut, burning through his resolve and patience. When Ben walked into the storage room he'd woken up in and explained his position, Walter had been calm. Agreeable, even. He'd gone along with the decision to bring him to the farm where they could confirm his veracity.

But standing out in the freezing temperatures, shaking not from the cold but from pure fury... It did things to a man.

Bad things.

Walter turned to Ben. "My wife needs medical attention. She's bleeding through an Israeli bandage on her arm."

Ben nodded to Daniel. "Is that true?"

"She's been shot."

Walter seethed. "Dani is unconscious. If she dies, I can't control what happens next." He glanced at Colt. "The man you caught will be the least of your problems."

"Are you insinuating more of your people will come?"

"Damn straight." Larkin spat on the ground. "And they won't be so hospitable."

Ben's nostrils flared. "Take the injured women to the medical facility. The other one can go with the men to the stables."

Craig hurried up to Dani and scooped her body into his arms. She flopped like a rag doll as he double-timed it out of sight.

Walter swallowed. "I need to be with my wife."

Ben thought it over, glancing between him, Larkin, and Colt, still unconscious on the ground. "All right."

Walter turned and followed Daniel around the stable to a building he'd never seen. Made of concrete block painted brown, it hugged the slope of the land up into the foothills at the rear of the farm.

Daniel shifted Tracy's weight and knocked on the door. It opened a moment later. A woman Walter didn't know ushered them inside.

"Take her to the triage area. The other girl is in the main room."

Walter glanced around. The place was set up like a small family doctor. Desk, cabinets for supplies, a cot in the corner, and a swinging door to a room beyond. They had spent more time outfitting this place than the barn.

Must expect a lot of injuries.

Walter waited as Daniel carried Tracy to the cot and laid her down. Only then did he approach. *Oh, Tracy.* He reached out and pulled her hair off her face, revealing a swollen, purple bruise on her temple. *Bastards.*

Her left arm dangled off the side of the cot and Walter picked it up. The bandage was soaked with blood. He didn't know how long he stood there, cradling his wife's arm and willing her to wake up, but his legs grew stiff and his back ached when he moved.

"Excuse me." The voice made him jump. "I need to check her vitals." The same woman who let them inside eased between him and his wife.

"I'm her husband."

She nodded and placed the stethoscope on Tracy's chest. "I'm Heather. Before everything fell apart, I was a nurse practitioner." She moved the stethoscope around, listening. "Your wife's breathing is normal. That's a good sign."

Walter stepped back and let her do her job, checking temperature and pupil dilation before inspecting the bandage. "Craig said it was most likely a 9mm. With this much blood, probably a through-and-through, but I'll need to take the bandage off to be sure."

"How's Dani?"

"The other girl?" Heather hesitated. "She's touch and go. Heart rate is steady, but weak. She lost a fair amount of blood. But the bullet missed the femoral by a few inches. She's lucky."

Walter snorted. "Not what I would call it."

Heather's lips thinned. "It will take a while for her body to replenish all the blood she lost. We're not equipped for transfusions here."

"But she'll live?"

"Probably."

Walter rubbed his face. He needed to find Colt and tell him the good news. "And my wife?"

"She'll be fine. If the bleeding has stopped, we'll need to bandage the wound but leave it open to drain."

"Otherwise infection will set in."

Heather softened. "Exactly. Now if you'll excuse me, I have work to do."

Walter stepped back and let Heather set to work cutting the bandage off Tracy's arm and cleaning the wound. The door opened behind him and Walter turned around.

Ben Jacobson. Walter frowned. The man was a conundrum. On the one hand, he let Walter stay at the farm free and unencumbered. On the other hand, he wouldn't let him leave. With Colt, Dani, and Larkin showing up and attempting a forcible rescue, Walter wasn't sure what would happen next.

But first, they would have some words. He stepped forward. "What on earth is going on here?"

Ben's eyes narrowed, deepening the wrinkles in the corners. "You tell me."

"I've cooperated with you the entire time I've been here. Hell, even before that when I woke up zip-tied in a root cellar."

"We didn't know who you were or if you were trustworthy."

Walter stood his ground. "The only proof I have that your men didn't shoot me is your word."

Ben exhaled and rubbed the short hairs on his chin. "I told you the truth. We found you out there, face-first in the snow. We thought you were alone."

"And when I told you I wasn't, you should have let me leave."

With heavy steps, Ben closed the distance between them, his eyes roaming past Walter to Heather and Tracy still unconscious on the gurney. "We take our safety extremely seriously."

Walter clenched a fist in frustration. "You've got to give me more than that. I thought you were interested in forming a friendship."

"This doesn't look like friendship."

"Neither does shooting my wife."

Ben took the criticism in stride, walking over to the

bank of cabinets and back again. They were at a stalemate and both men knew it.

Walter offered the first branch. "I appreciate you rescuing me from the snow and the rehab Heather has done to my shoulder, but what happened tonight isn't okay." He paused to choose his words carefully. "I told you my family would be looking for me."

"Your wife wasn't looking for you."

Walter blinked. "What are you talking about? She was at the hospital, searching for me."

Ben shook his head. "She wasn't looking for you. She broke into the pharmacy at the hospital. She was looking for drugs."

Walter staggered back. It didn't make sense. "The pharmacy? What do you have to do with it?"

Ben rubbed the back of his neck, debating what to say.

Walter pressed him. "I deserve the truth. My wife is shot. Dani might as well be family and she could die."

At last, Ben conceded. "We control the pharmacy. It was one of the first things we did."

"I don't understand." Walter squinted like he couldn't see. "Are you drug runners?"

"No. We're maintaining the medicine supply for when the country gets back on its feet."

Walter reeled. All this time there had been an intact pharmacy in the middle of town and he'd never known. They had avoided the hospital because they knew it was hopeless. He thought back to Chico State and the disaster they confronted there only a few days after the

EMP. Every broken and destroyed pharmacy they drove past on their way to Truckee. The riots in Sacramento.

And here this collection of families were holding down an entire hospital pharmacy just for safekeeping. He didn't know whether to laugh or punch Ben in the face. But none of it had anything to do with Tracy.

"So why was my wife there?"

Ben rolled his eyes. "According to Daniel, she claimed to be looking for a rabies vaccine."

Walter's stomach lurched. "What for?"

"She said your daughter was infected. But we know that's a lie."

Walter swallowed flecks of spit. "You do?"

Ben snorted. "Of course. She looks just fine."

"Madison is here?" Walter surged forward. "Where? Why didn't you tell me?"

"You saw her. She was carted in with your wife." Ben stared at him like he'd confessed to being an alien. "The blonde," he waved at his head, "with the hair."

The pit in Walter's stomach opened and he fought the urge to strangle Ben with his bare hands. "That's not my daughter. That's Brianna. Her family owns the farm we live at." He cupped the back of his head and tried not to panic. "Madison is my daughter. Brown hair, my nose, same coloring as her mother."

Ben stared at him, his expression grim.

"I take it she's not here."

Ben strode over to Heather who still worked patiently by Tracy's side. While Walter and Ben talked, she had removed the bandage and cleaned the wound.

"How is she?"

"Not bad. The girl did a good job securing the bandage. Minimal blood loss. With a round of antibiotics, the wound should heal just fine." She glanced at Walter with an apologetic smile. "She might have a scar."

Ben nodded. "And the other one?"

Heather's smile faded. "Touch and go."

He turned back to Walter. "Stay here with your wife. I'll be back soon."

"Where are you going?"

"To figure out what to do." Ben pushed the door open, leaving a rush of cold in his wake.

Walter turned back to his wife. Brown hair fading into gray at the temples. Skin hardened by a year working in the fields. Hands covered in calluses. Even unconscious, she was the most beautiful woman he'd ever seen.

He would stay by her side until she woke up and told him about their daughter. He glanced at Heather. "Looks like I'm here for a while. What can I do to help?"

CHAPTER TWENTY-THREE

COLT

Unidentified Farm
  Near Truckee, CA
  12:00 p.m.

Between the horse crap caking his boots and the epic fail of a rescue mission, Colt had stepped in it every way possible. He pounded his fist into his palm and kept pacing.

He woke up an hour ago, sprawled out on a stack of hay bales in a stable. With whinnying horses on his left and bleating sheep on his right, he'd fit right in. A caged animal just waiting for his chance to strike.

Larkin was unaccounted for, Tracy, Brianna, and Walter were nowhere to be seen, and Dani could be dead by now. If any of them ended up dying because of him...

Colt shook his head. He should have taken the leader out when he had the chance. The sight of those kids had turned him soft. Weak. He pressed his fingers to his eyelids.

"Hello? Is anyone in here? Hello?"

Colt lifted his head. He recognized that voice. "Brianna? Is that you?"

"Colt? What are you doing here?" Something rattled down the barn. "Where is here?"

He snorted. "If you couldn't tell, we're at a farm."

"I guessed that by the smell."

"And the shit." A man's voice called out from opposite Colt's stall. "Don't forget that."

"Larkin?"

"The one and only."

Colt strode to the front of the stable and gripped the wood gate. Brianna's curls stuck through the posts three stables down and Larkin's hands dangled out from the one straight across. "Are we the only ones here?"

"Looks that way." Larkin stepped back. "I haven't seen Walter."

Colt's jaw ticked. "What about Tracy and Dani?"

"No sign of them. Wherever they took them, it wasn't here."

"Would you two stop acting like it's just another day in the neighborhood and help a girl out? I'm clueless."

Colt smiled despite his mood. "We tracked Walter here. It's a farm that seems to be run by a few families."

"So how did we end up in the stables?"

"We're here because I failed in the rescue mission."

Larkin interrupted. "We failed."

Colt's jaw ticked. He refused to put the blame on

anyone but himself. "You all showed up unconscious in a pickup truck right when everything was going to hell."

"It doesn't make any sense." Brianna huffed and Colt could imagine her pacing back and forth, trying to figure it out. "We were at the hospital."

"Why?"

"You saw Madison's injury. She needs a vaccine."

Colt wrinkled his nose. "For a cut?"

"A bite. A fox bit her while she was inspecting the traps. It tested positive for rabies."

"Crap." Colt ran a hand down his face. "How long ago?"

"Long enough to make every minute count. We had no luck at the vet's office on the edge of town so we went straight to the hospital." Her voice lightened. "You should have seen it. The pharmacy was pristine. Not a single shelf disturbed."

"Are you sure you didn't hit your head?" Larkin's tone matched Colt's thoughts. "Every pharmacy is trashed by now."

"Not this one. It was under guard. We thought we could get in and out and not be seen, but it didn't work out that way."

Colt couldn't believe it. The farm was more than just a family trying to survive. If they were the same people who organized runs out of the warehouse where Lottie tracked Walter and were guarding the hospital pharmacy, it was a bigger operation that Colt realized.

He strained to see outside the barn, but the stable walls limited his view to about fifteen feet. How many people did it take to maintain security at a pharmacy, go on regular raids, and keep a farm of this size working?

The horse in the stall next to Colt began to stamp and neigh and he pulled away from the gate. Footsteps sounded on the hard-packed dirt.

"Easy, girl, easy. I know they smell like strangers, but it's okay."

Colt recognized the voice and surged forward. "What did you do with Dani? Is she still alive?"

The man identified as Ben walked into view. He rested a shotgun on his shoulder and his brow knit as he spotted Colt. He opened his mouth to answer when Brianna threw something at the gate. A burst of something thick and sludgy flew through the slats and landed on Ben's foot.

Colt knew what it was from the smell and he bit his tongue to keep from laughing.

Ben stepped out of range. "Let's lay off the crap-throwing, shall we?"

"Not until you let me out of here, you son of a bitch! My best friend is going to die because of you! All we wanted was a damn vaccine!"

"My men assessed the situation and believed you were there for drugs."

"Who died and appointed you king?"

"No one. But we aren't going to let the neighborhood meth heads ruin everything." He glanced at Colt. "We aren't the bad guys here."

"You sure are acting like it." Brianna refused to give up. She launched another glob of horse manure through the bars. It missed Ben by a foot. "What are you saving all the drugs for, anyway? To launch a new business? A new drug cartel? Are illegal drugs not good enough now that no one can even find an antibiotic?"

"We aren't drug dealers. We're protectors. At some point, the chaos will die down and America will rebuild. We'll need the medicine."

Brianna shrieked in frustration. "Madison needs a rabies vaccine and she needs it right now! Screw rebuilding. If everyone dies because you're trying out for an episode of *Hoarders*, I swear to God you'll regret it."

"I'm beginning to already." Ben exhaled and lapsed into silence.

Colt tried again. "Tell me about Dani. Is she still alive?"

"It's touch and go."

"I want to see her."

Ben shook his head. "No."

"I want proof of life."

"You'll have to take my word for it."

Colt spun around in a circle and punched at the closest bale of hay. If he had to kill every stranger in the place to find her, he would. No one was keeping him from saving that girl. If she was still alive, then he was getting her out of there.

He focused on the shotgun still resting on the man's shoulder. The farm had an arsenal, that much was plain. And from everything he'd seen, every adult carried at least one weapon.

Even if he did escape, all it would take was one

person spotting him and it would be over. He didn't doubt the orders this time were to kill. Colt ground his teeth together. He couldn't rescue Dani without firepower.

He sucked in a huge breath and let it out slow enough to calm his frantic heart. "How about we call a truce? You let us out of the animal pens and we can all have a chat like civilized people."

"Are you crazy?" Brianna stormed inside her stable. "We're wasting time."

Ben turned to Colt. "I'm listening."

"We're unarmed. You've got Tracy and Dani as basically hostages. Let's take a step back and talk about this like men."

"And women!" Brianna kicked the gate and her whole stable shook.

"You promise to stand down?"

Colt stuck his hand through the slats. "On my honor."

Ben hesitated for a moment before shaking his hand. "All right. But I'm keeping armed guards. And you can't see the other women until we've reached an agreement."

Colt nodded. He didn't care what lies he had to tell. He would agree to sell his first-born child, everyone back home, and all their guns, just to get a chance to take the big man down. He stepped back as Ben walked toward the end of the barn.

"Daniel! Craig! Come escort our guests to the bunkhouse. They can shower and get cleaned up. Loan them some clothes." Ben turned back to Colt. "Once you're all cleaned up, I'll have food delivered to your rooms. You won't be able to go anywhere without an escort and you can't leave the bunkhouse without my permission. Is that clear?"

"Crystal."

Colt waited while the guards came in to unlock the stable gates. They pointed what looked to be Army-issued M-4s in their direction. Even if Colt got the upper hand, he wouldn't be able to disarm two men with the ability to fire thirty rounds in bursts of three. He would have to wait for another chance.

In the meantime, he could do some much-needed reconnaissance. Brianna stepped out into the aisle and waited under guard while the second man let Colt out. As Colt stepped closer to Brianna, he took a whiff. "You stink."

She leaned in. "As bad as I smell, this whole situation will stink a lot worse if you don't know what you're doing."

The guards closed in and Colt plastered on a smile. He waited until Larkin was released before nodding at his old friend. "Let's get cleaned up and then we'll have a chance to relax."

Brianna's eyes sparked with anger, but Larkin cut her a glance to stay quiet. It would be difficult to plan if they were never left alone, but he would find a way. They would find the rest of their friends and get out of there one way or another.

In the interim, he hoped to make Ben pay.

CHAPTER TWENTY-FOUR

TRACY

Jacobson Family Farmhouse
  Near Truckee, CA
  2:00 p.m.

The first thing Tracy saw when she opened her eyes was her husband's face. Her mouth fell open. "I'm dead, aren't I?"

Walter laughed. "No, honey. You're very much alive." He bent down to kiss her forehead and Tracy snuffed back a wave of tears.

"I thought I was a goner." She lifted her arm and pain lanced her bicep. Vertigo washed over her as sweat broke out across her forehead. "Definitely not dead."

Her husband helped her sit up and she took in her surroundings for the first time. It was a makeshift medical facility. She frowned. "Are we still in the hospital?"

"No. We're at a farm."

She gripped her husband's arm. "Madison is in trouble! We need a vaccine."

"I know."

"Then why aren't you worried?"

"I am, but it's complicated." Walter glanced at the door. "There's a lot that's happened."

"Tell me."

Walter perched on the edge of the cot and relayed everything that happened since he was shot in the street.

When he finished, Tracy sat quietly for a minute, piecing the information together. "So the family that controls the pharmacy found you on the street, fixed you up, but won't let you leave?"

"That's the short version."

"And now they're refusing to give Madison the vaccine."

Walter scratched behind his ear. "I wouldn't say refuse."

"But they haven't agreed."

"Correct."

Tracy exhaled. "This is ridiculous. One look at us and they should know we aren't a bunch of drug users hell-bent on destroying the pharmacy. It's not like we're asking for painkillers. We need a *vaccine*."

Walter ran his thumb over the back of Tracy's hand. "It gets worse." He glanced past her to an interior door. "Colt, Larkin, and Dani tried to rescue me."

"What happened?"

"Dani was shot."

"Where is she?" Tracy scrambled off the cot, but her

legs wobbled as she tried to stand. Walter caught her before she hit the ground.

"Easy. You need to rest."

"I need to see her." Tracy gripped her husband by the forearms to keep upright. "Where's Colt? Does he know?"

"They took him, Brianna, and Larkin to the stables. I'm assuming they're still there."

"Not anymore." A man stood in the doorway to the medical facility, his massive shoulders blotting out the view of the farm beyond. "They are in the bunkhouse getting cleaned up."

The man strode forward and stretched out his hand. "Ben Jacobson. Good to see you up and on your feet."

Tracy shook his hand with caution. "Tracy Sloane. You know about my daughter, Madison?"

"Yes."

"Then you know we need a vaccine as soon as possible. Every second we delay, she's at risk. If we don't get to her before the virus reaches her central nervous system..."

"It will be too late. I'm aware." He turned to Walter. "I've spoken with Colt. He's agreed to stand down in exchange for a conversation about where we go from here."

Tracy stamped her foot and the room spun. "That's not good enough and you know it."

"You have to give us more than that, Ben." Walter hugged Tracy closer. "She's our only daughter."

The other man held up a hand. "I'm prepared to give

you all the benefit of the doubt. We will give you the vaccine."

Tracy clutched her husband to keep from falling. "Thank God."

"But it comes with conditions."

"We're listening."

"First, you give us directions to your farm. Three of my men will go there with the vaccine. I've instructed them they cannot leave until they have a visual on Madison and confirm that she is sick. Only then will they hand over the vaccine."

Walter shook his head. "That will never work. The Cliftons will shoot them before they even enter the gate."

"My men can defend themselves."

Tracy rolled her eyes. "So you're going to go all *Call of Duty* out in the woods? What for? To make a point?" She pulled away from Walter and stood on her own two feet. "If we don't go with you, it's a lost cause."

Ben's lips thinned into a line. His brown eyes bounced back and forth, assessing Tracy and Walter. "One of you can go."

"Not good enough. We need two."

"Fine. I'll get the blonde." Ben glanced at his shoes. "She's proving to be a pain in the neck around here."

Tracy bit back a grin. "What about Walter?"

"He stays."

Tracy nibbled on her cheek. They were risking their lives trusting a man who was essentially keeping them prisoner, but they didn't have a choice. Ben had access to a vaccine. She pulled her husband aside.

"Will you be okay here on your own?"

"Colt and Larkin will be here, too." He stroked her hair. "What about you and Brianna? It's risky."

"We have to do it. Once her parents spot her, Brianna can convince them to let everyone in." She squeezed her husband's hand. "It's the best way."

"I don't like you going on your own."

"I don't like leaving you, but Madison needs us." Tracy planted a quick kiss on Walter's cheek and stepped away. "Everything will work out." She turned to Ben. "When do we leave?"

"Within the hour."

* * *

2:30 p.m.

"This is ridiculous." Brianna lifted both hands behind her head and pulled her wet hair back into a French braid. "My parents are liable to shoot us before we even get near the gate."

"Then you better convince them not to." Daniel, one of Ben's henchmen, scowled as he climbed into the driver's seat of a Chevy Silverado on a lift kit. "I'm not interested in bleeding out today."

Brianna finished her hair before climbing onto a tire and over the side of the bed. She flopped onto a blanket-covered hay bale and crossed her arms. "You might as well drive up with a banner that says *We're The Bad*

Guys all over it. No way will my Dad think I'm in the back of this thing via my own free will."

"What's wrong with it?" Craig, one of their other escorts, leaned back to look at the truck before climbing in the front seat.

"It's not the truck that's the problem. It's the occupants."

Walter helped Tracy into the bed and squeezed her hand. "I'll see you again soon." He smiled and leaned close. "Keep that one out of trouble."

Tracy glanced at Brianna. "I don't think that's possible, but I'll try."

Walter pulled back and slapped the side of the truck. It rumbled to life.

Tracy settled into a spot on the wall of the bed, using a hay bale as a back rest. She motioned to Brianna. "How about you relax for a bit?"

"Not a chance." The younger woman pouted. "They're just waiting to get out of view before they shoot us in the head and dump our bodies in a ditch."

"No, they aren't."

The truck jostled over the gravel drive and Brianna slid down to the floor to keep from falling out. She twisted her hands in her lap, reminding Tracy that she was only twenty. She looked up, the first hint of fear in her face. "How can you be so sure?"

"Because they want to scope out the farm first. They won't kill us until we get them inside."

Brianna snorted. "And here I thought you'd bought into their lies."

Tracy shrugged. "I haven't made up my mind. They could have killed us back at the hospital and dumped our bodies along with the rest of them in the morgue. But they didn't."

"You said it yourself, it's so they can find out what we have."

"Or else it's because they thought we might be telling the truth." She nodded up at the cab. "They have the vaccine. I watched Ben hand it to Daniel before we left."

The truck bounced around a curve and Brianna slid into the middle. "If we can overpower them, we can take the vaccine and get home alone."

Tracy shook her head. "Us against three guys who probably played football at UN Reno? We don't stand a chance." Tracy reached out and gave Brianna's leg a pat. "For now, we play along. Convince your parents to let us in, give Madison the vaccine, and then—"

"All bets are off."

"Exactly." Tracy leaned back on the hay bale and closed her eyes. Every time she moved her left arm, shooting pain arced through her flesh to her fingers and up over her shoulder blade.

"You okay?"

She blinked her eyes open. "I will be once I know Madison is okay."

"I meant your arm."

Tracy smiled. "It'll heal. How about you?" Tracy pointed at a goose egg on the side of Brianna's head. "They hit you pretty hard to leave a lump like that."

The younger woman reached up and patted the

bruise, wincing as her fingers made contact. "I've had worse."

The pair lapsed into silence, each worried about Madison, the safety of the Clifton compound, and what would happen if their escorts turned out not to be telling the truth. Tracy wished she had a weapon. It wouldn't be a failsafe, but just having something to defend herself with would calm her nerves.

After half an hour, the truck slowed. Brianna leaned out and banged on the side of the door. The window rolled down. "Turn in, but don't go more than twenty feet down the drive. I'll have to walk the rest of the way on foot."

Craig turned around to face her. "Not alone you won't."

The truck rumbled to a stop and Craig and John hopped out. Brianna followed. One look at his rifle and she palmed her hips. "My parents see that and you're dead before you even catch a glimpse of a single cabin."

He glanced at Daniel. The other man handed over a pistol. Craig took it and set the rifle in the truck. "Fine, but no funny business. I can shoot you with a 9mm just as well." He glanced up at Tracy and almost grinned. "Just ask her."

Brianna strode forward and stamped on his foot. Craig jumped back, cursing and hopping as he grabbed his toes.

"Don't be a dick. My parents will shoot you for that, too." She took off, stomping down the gravel road and Tracy couldn't help but laugh.

Daniel stared at the empty spot where Craig and Brianna used to be. "My brother's got his hands full." He glanced at Tracy. "Is she always like that?"

Tracy shook her head as she tried to breathe. "Most of the time, she's worse."

CHAPTER TWENTY-FIVE

COLT

Unidentified Farm
Near Truckee, CA
3:00 p.m.

"Something's going on. I can feel it." Colt ran his hand over his hair and rolled his shoulders. The sweater they gave him itched like new wool.

Larkin sat at one of the desks, scooping peanut butter out of a jar. "They wouldn't let us shower and feed us if they were planning on killing us. Relax." He shoved a spoonful into his mouth and groaned. "I haven't had Jif in years. I forgot how good it was."

"Dani could be dead and you're slobbering over peanut butter. Your priorities are seriously messed up."

"She's not dead. And if she is," Larkin paused to lick a blob off his finger, "there's nothing we can do about it. You should eat."

"I should find a way to kill everyone in this place, is what I should do. Definitely not eat. For all you know, that jar is laced with poison. You could be foaming at the mouth in minutes."

Larkin shrugged. "There are worse ways to go."

"Jesus." Colt sat down hard in the other desk chair. Larkin was right. They couldn't do anything trapped inside a bunk room with an armed guard standing watch outside. If Dani was dead, then nothing else mattered. If she was still alive, he needed his strength to save her.

He held out his hand. "Pass me the jar."

"Atta boy." Larkin handed over the peanut butter and another spoon.

Colt took a bite and closed his eyes. It was damn good. He remembered how amazing food tasted whenever he returned home from missions years ago. After months in the desert, simple things like a piece of bread with butter could almost make him cry.

Larkin cleared his throat. "You need me to give you some privacy with that jar?"

Colt leaned back with a laugh. "Thanks for talking me off the ledge."

"Don't go getting all soft. I wanted you to eat, not give up." Larkin stood up and carried his chair close enough to whisper. "You remember that gag we pulled at Walter Reed with the visiting nurse on the night shift?"

"The brunette with the legs for days?" Colt stared up at the ceiling. "What was her name?"

"Victoria."

He grinned, remembering her face when she found

out it was a false alarm. "I sure do. But what's that got to do with anything?"

"I figure if it fools a nurse, it ought to fool a football player."

Colt glanced at the door. "How are we going to disarm him?"

Larkin held up a pair of shoelaces tied together. "All we need is a few seconds."

Colt clapped Larkin on the back. "It's good to have you around." He finished off the peanut butter and put the lid on the jar while Larkin moved his chair back into position.

It only took a few minutes to plan the attack. When they were ready, Larkin held one hand out in front of him. "I've got two pencils. Whoever is left with the shortest one has to be the victim."

Colt plucked one.

Larkin opened his hand. "Aw, man. If I throw up, I'm aiming for your shoes."

Colt walked over to the door and waited, doubled shoelace balled up in his fist.

Larkin sucked in a breath and crawled onto the floor. He clutched at his throat.

Colt banged on the door. "Help! Help! I think he's choking!"

Larkin's face turned red as he forced himself not to breathe.

Colt hit the door harder. "He's going to die! Help!"

The door opened and the single guard eyed him warily.

Colt pointed at Larkin, now a violent shade of purple on the floor. "He's choking!"

The guard rushed in and Colt followed close behind. "You know the Heimlich?"

Colt shook his head. "No! Can't you do something? Look at him!"

Larkin's eyes were bugging out of his face. If he didn't breathe soon, he would pass out. Colt shouted louder. "Do something!"

The guard leaned over, arms outstretched, rifle dangling from his shoulder. It was the best chance Colt was going to get. He unfurled the shoelace and crowded up against his back.

As the man began to stand, Colt whipped the cord around his neck and yanked. He was outweighed by at least twenty pounds, but Colt had determination on his side. While Larkin sucked in oxygen, gasping like a fish on a dock, Colt tightened the cord.

The guard grunted and clawed at the shoelace, but Colt hung on. He counted in his head. *Five. Six. Seven.* If he had a good enough hold, the guy should pass out within fifteen seconds.

It took twenty. The guard sagged and Colt grabbed the rifle before letting the shoelace go.

Larkin eked out words between gulps of air. "D-Did you kill him?"

"I hope not." Colt used the shoelace to tie the man's wrists to the bunk bed's post. The guy would wake up soon. He glanced at Larkin. "You okay?"

Larkin nodded. His face had almost returned to

normal. He picked up the rifle and switched the safety off. "The nurse was easier."

"We didn't choke her."

"Next time, it's your turn."

Colt grabbed his coat and hurried to the door. "Come on. He'll wake up any second." Most blood chokes lasted less than a minute. They didn't have much time.

With Larkin following on his heels, Colt poked his head around the open door. The hall was empty. "Brianna must be in one of these rooms."

Larkin held out the rifle. "I'll stay here and look for Brianna. You go find Dani."

Colt glanced at the gun. "You'll be defenseless."

Larkin tapped his head. "Not entirely. Now go."

Colt nodded once and took off down the hall, away from the rec room and toward the antechamber he'd first entered the day before. Somewhere on the farm, Dani was locked away and he was determined to find her.

CHAPTER TWENTY-SIX

WALTER

Jacobson Family Farmhouse
   Near Truckee, CA
   3:00 p.m.

"Thank you for sending the vaccine to my daughter." Walter leaned back and sipped the hot coffee Ben brewed moments before.

"You're welcome." He set his own mug on the table and leaned back. "I feel I owe you an apology. We should have listened when you said your family would come looking." He ran a hand down his beard. "I honestly thought when we picked you up that you were delusional. Maybe had a bit of Alzheimer's."

"Do I look that old already?"

"You have a bit of the crazy old guy vibe, yeah."

"Guess I should listen to my wife when she says I

need a haircut." Walter grew somber and leaned forward. "I'm sorry we met under these circumstances. It seems that we're out for the same things."

"To rebuild America."

"And stay alive in the process."

Ben held out his mug and Walter clinked his against it. The door behind Ben opened and a little girl of about eight rushed in, braids waving behind her and hood flopping against her back. She stopped beside Ben, panting and out of breath.

"Daddy! Daddy, I saw a dog in the field."

Ben hugged his daughter before pointing at Walter. "We're in the middle of a grown-up talk, sweetie. Can you tell me about it later?"

"But Daddy, I want to keep it."

"Stray dogs are dangerous, you know that, Wendy."

"Mr. Larkin says it's his dog." She pouted and stamped a foot. "But I want to keep it."

Ben glanced at Walter. "What do you mean, Mr. Larkin?"

"I was coming here to tell you." Jenny, Ben's wife, walked in and nodded at Walter. "It seems we've had a bit of a jailbreak."

Larkin eased in past the woman and Ben began to stand. Jenny waved him off. "It's okay, Benjamin. We've talked. He's a good man."

Ben eased back down. "Is that so?"

Larkin scratched behind his ear. "Halfway decent, at least."

Walter chuckled. "Don't let his humility fool you.

He's saved my life more than once and we only met after the EMP."

"Jenny tells me that you've sent Brianna and Tracy with the vaccine to the Cliftons' place."

"That's right."

Larkin nodded. "Good."

Ben motioned to the bench. "With the crisis averted and my wife deeming you acceptable, come and sit. We can talk about next steps."

Larkin scratched his head again and glanced behind him. "That's just it. The crisis isn't over. Not one hundred percent."

Walter swallowed. "Let me guess."

"Colt's out there and he's on a mission."

Ben stood up. "Jenny, get Wendy and the rest of the kids inside."

"But Daddy, what about the dog?"

"Not now, sweetie. Do what I said. Go to Mommy." He gave his daughter a pat and reached for his pistol.

"Do you really think that's necessary?"

"That man tried to kill me while on the ground and defenseless." He checked the chamber. "I should be carrying a bazooka." Ben turned to Larkin. "Where's the last place you saw him?"

Larkin exhaled. "Leaving the bunk rooms. He was looking for Dani."

Ben pushed past Larkin and out the door.

Walter stood up. "We better get out there. Ben's liable to shoot first and not bother to ask a damn thing."

"Then God help him, because he won't stand a chance."

CHAPTER TWENTY-SEVEN

TRACY

Clifton Compound
    Near Truckee, CA
    4:00 p.m.

A shiver racked Tracy's frame and she rose up onto her toes to peer over the hood of the truck. "Any chance we can get inside?"

Daniel blew warm air into his hands. "I'll catch holy hell from Ben if I do."

"Why? You've got someone on patrol. I don't have a weapon. No one's going to be happy if we freeze to death."

After a moment, he relented and tugged open the driver's door. "Get in. I'll turn the engine on for a few minutes to warm it up."

Tracy climbed up and fell into the passenger seat. As soon as the first hint of heat spread from the vents, she pulled off her gloves and warmed her hands. "Thank you. I was close to frostbite."

He nodded. About Madison's age, Daniel had a quiet way about him. He reminded Tracy of Peyton. A kind giant. She glanced at the rifle. Even the gentle ones had to fight now.

"Are you from here?"

He jerked up, her question bringing alarm to his eyes.

She held up her hands. "Just making conversation."

He twisted in the seat and leaned his wide shoulders against the window. "Yeah. Born and raised. Ben is my uncle."

Tracy nodded. She could see the resemblance in the blocky head and square frame. "Did you always want to be a farmer?"

"Not a chance." He laughed and the tension eased from his neck. "I was in school to be a landscape architect."

"Really?"

"University of Nevada, Reno. Two years left when it all... ended."

Tracy swallowed. "You're the same age as my daughter."

"Was she there, too? I might know her."

Tracy shook her head. "We're from California. She was at UC Davis, studying agriculture."

They fell into easy conversation about the Clifton property and Madison's work clearing the ground for their first farm. Then it was on to Anne's skills canning and preserving and Brianna's knack for getting into trouble.

Daniel's eyes brightened the more Tracy talked. "You guys sound like us." He smiled at the seat. "Ben's always saying Craig talks too much for his own good and Heather's too softhearted."

"Is she the nurse?"

He nodded. "My older sister."

"Where are your parents?"

Daniel's face fell. "They were on vacation when the lights went out. Their first cruise." He looked out the window. "I like to think they're still in the Bahamas, oblivious to all of this here."

Tracy nodded. She'd lost a lot of people, too. "So why the pharmacy?"

Daniel looked up, trying to put together the words. "Ben thinks this is all temporary. That as soon as the government is up and running again, the country will put itself back together."

"So you're protecting the pharmacy for the future?"

"He says hospitals will need medicine and doctors and researchers will use what we save to create more."

Tracy ran a hand through her hair. "What if that doesn't happen? What if the government never comes back?"

Daniel chewed on his lip. "I don't know. I guess it's all ours."

She nodded and looked away. They seemed like good people, but Ben was either delusional or naive. The government wouldn't rebuild. At least not in the way he thought. Even if people in Washington, DC were putting their lives back together, how long before word reached the West Coast?

A year? Two? Ten?

By then new governments would form. People would cobble together new communities and towns. Walter even heard on the radio that someone was trying to get steam locomotives up and running. It would be a new industrial revolution with supply lines powered by what made America great two hundred years before.

She tried to smile at Daniel. "I hope Ben is right and we do rebuild."

"But you don't think it'll happen?"

Tracy chose her words carefully. "Over the past nine months, I've seen some of the worst humanity has to offer. I'm not sure we can go back to what we had before."

Daniel's face fell.

Tracy hated to be the bearer of depressing news. She reached out and patted his shoulder. "But I hope it does. You're doing a good thing with the farm."

He nodded. "Sometimes, when I'm asleep, I dream of the world the way it was before. I'm sitting in my dorm room, snarfing down a delivery pizza, playing Xbox with one of my friends." He faltered. "Then I wake up and I realize it wasn't real."

Tracy knew exactly what he meant. She still dreamt of their house in Sacramento, sipping tea on the back porch and waiting for her husband to come home. Then there were the harder dreams: watching Madison graduate from college, a wedding, grandchildren. A future.

She swallowed.

Daniel pointed at the road. "Is that one of yours?"

An ATV came barreling down the snow-covered gravel, flinging rocks in its wake. Tracy nodded. "That's Brianna. They must be done."

Tracy clambered down out of the truck and the cold air stole her breath. She couldn't wait for spring.

Brianna stopped the ATV ten feet from the truck and put it in park before climbing out. "I talked my parents out of shooting anyone, although they thought about making an example out of me for a minute." She grinned and kept talking. "We're welcome to come in."

"And the vaccine?" Tracy turned to Daniel.

He nodded. "It's all yours."

Tracy exhaled. *Finally*. She hurried to climb in the back of the truck. Daniel honked and John appeared out of the tree line. Together, the three of them followed Brianna back to the Cliftons' home.

It took five minutes to bump down the drive, hop out, and find Madison in the cabin where she left her in what felt like a lifetime before. She smiled.

"Hi, Mom."

"How are you, honey?" Tracy rushed to her daughter's side.

"Good." Madison stuck out her leg. "It's healing."

The bite had shriveled into a prune-shaped scab. Tracy turned to Daniel.

He held a box out to Tracy. "It's four doses. The standard protocol for post-bite inoculation."

She took it with gratitude in her heart. "Thank you."

After reading the instructions, she pulled up Madison's sleeve. "This is going to hurt."

Her daughter braced herself and Tracy sank the needle deep before plunging. The vaccine disappeared into Madison's arm and Tracy exhaled. She felt like she'd held her breath for two days.

"When will we know if it worked?"

Tracy turned to Brianna who stood nearby, watching. The young woman shook her head. "I don't know. I guess when she doesn't get symptoms?"

"According to the directions, you get another dose at day three, seven, and fourteen."

Madison tilted her head toward Daniel. "Who's he?"

In her rush to inject her daughter, Tracy forgot she didn't know anything about the past fifty-four hours. "He's from a nearby farm." Tracy waved him over. "Daniel Jacobson, meet Madison Sloane, my daughter."

He stuck out an awkward hand and Madison shook it. "Pleased to meet you."

"Thanks to his uncle, we got the medicine."

Brianna crossed her arms. "You mean in spite of."

Madison's head swiveled as she looked first at Brianna and then Tracy. "Is there something more to the story?"

Tracy stood up. "We can fill you in later. Right now you need to rest." She fluffed Madison's pillow and waited until she lay back down before turning to

Brianna. "Let's all meet in the cook cabin. We should talk."

Brianna glowered at Daniel. "Him, too?"

"Everyone." Tracy motioned for Daniel to join her and together they stepped out into the trampled snow. She zipped up her jacket and pointed at the main cabin used for cooking. "Let's all meet here. You, Craig, John, and all of us."

He kicked at the snow. "What for?"

She waited until he looked up, and she smiled. "Because I think this could be the start of something beneficial for everyone. It would be a shame to waste it."

Daniel rubbed his hair. "Ben should be the one to make that decision."

"I know. But you should have a voice in the matter, too." Tracy knew if she convinced the younger Jacobson, it would carry weight with his uncle. How much, she wasn't sure. But it never hurt to try.

Tracy was tired of always thinking the worst of others, never relying on anyone except their tight-knit little group. Ten people in the middle of the forest couldn't rebuild a single town let alone the United States. It would take banding together.

Ben Jacobson might not be perfect, but he was the best option they had come across in nine months. She wouldn't give up until he either categorically refused or the Cliftons walked away.

Daniel walked over to the truck where his brother and cousin waited and Tracy headed inside the cook cabin. Anne and Barry stood in the window, watching.

She smiled at them both. "There's a few gentlemen here that I'd like you to meet."

Barry nodded without a hint of a smile. "Brianna says they can't be trusted."

Tracy exhaled. "I think they can. It's early yet, but they're doing something special. We should think about an alliance."

Anne leaned into her husband. "Let's at least meet them. We can always make up our minds later."

"Fine." Barry turned and set his mug on the counter. "But we're not agreeing to anything until we meet the head of their operation."

Tracy agreed. "That sounds fair." She stepped back outside and ushered the boys in. "Come on in, fellas. Meet the Cliftons."

CHAPTER TWENTY-EIGHT

COLT

Unidentified Farm
    Near Truckee, CA
    4:00 p.m.

Colt put himself in the shoes of a smug jerk like Ben and tried to figure out where Dani might be. So far, he was striking out. All the obvious choices turned out to be duds.

Creeping past a fence line separating one animal pen from another, he heard a yip. *Strange.* He hadn't seen any dogs on the property before. He shrugged. Maybe they were indoor dogs like Lottie.

Colt kept going. The barking intensified. All at once, a ball of brown and gray fluff skidded through the snow in front of him. The little thing jumped up and pawed his shins.

"Lottie?" Colt scooped up the little dog in amazement. "How'd you find me?"

One touch of her paws and he shoved his gun in his belt. "You're freezing." He rubbed her feet one at a time and tried to warm her up. She wasn't having it.

"What is it, girl?"

She wriggled out of his arms and back into the snow, but she didn't stay. Instead, she took off, barking and yipping and carrying on. Every few leaps, she turned to check if Colt was coming.

He didn't have the faintest clue what the dog was doing, but following her was better than wandering. Lottie scurried over clumps of melting snow to a concrete block building painted brown.

"It's a shed. You can't possibly want anything in there."

Lottie pawed and barked at the door.

Colt pushed it open, expecting a wall of tools. He found the opposite. "What on earth?"

He entered the room, frowning at the gurney and the chairs and the desk in the corner. Lottie barked for attention at a second door.

Colt hurried to open it. At the sight, he dropped his hand and the door almost swung shut on his face. *It can't be.* "Dani?"

Lottie leapt from the floor onto an empty chair, scrambled over to a bedside table, and up onto a hospital bed where Dani shrieked in glee.

A woman with dark hair pulled back in a ponytail

and eyes the same brown as Ben's turned around. "Who are you?"

Colt swallowed.

"It's okay. That's Colt." Dani ruffled Lottie's fur. "And this is Lottie." She laughed and Colt gripped the doorframe to keep from falling.

Dani is alive... and she's laughing. He almost forgot what it sounded like.

He stepped up to her. "How are you?"

"Good. A little woozy if I try to stand."

"Then don't." The woman stuck out her hand. "Heather Jacobson."

Colt hesitated. "Ben's wife?"

Her eyes went wide for a beat before she laughed. "No. Niece. God help me if I marry someone like him."

The anger and rage that he'd used to break free and find Dani melted like ice on a hot car. Heather wasn't anything like her uncle. He stuck out his hand and she shook it. "Pleased to meet you."

"I hear you're the troublemaker."

"Is that a problem?"

Heather's eyes flashed. "Not necessarily."

He ran a hand through his hair, suddenly off-kilter. It had been a long time since he'd talked to a woman he didn't know. Especially a pretty one. "Planning on turning me in?"

She laughed. "A guy who runs in with a five-pound dog and a grin a mile wide? Not a chance."

He protested. "She's seven pounds at least."

"Hello?" Dani leaned forward, waving her hands about. "Girl with a gunshot wound over here."

Colt turned. He had time to get to know Heather later. Dani would need rest and recuperation. He searched her small frame. "Where were you hit?"

"My thigh." Dani pulled down the covers and pointed at a large bandage. "Heather says a few inches over and I'd have bled out in minutes."

"It missed the femoral artery completely." Heather focused on the bed. "My brother felt terrible about it. Said he panicked."

Colt would deal with the shooter later. He was focused on Dani's recovery. "She lost a lot of blood. I thought—" He didn't finish.

"The snow and freezing temperatures helped. It slowed everything down. Her heart rate, the blood loss, all of it."

"Who knew snow was good for something?" Dani picked up Lottie's feet and frowned. "Where are her booties?"

"Back in the Jeep, probably."

"Didn't you get them?"

Colt shook his head. "I didn't go back for her. She found me." He smiled. "And you."

Dani picked up the little dog and nuzzled her face. "That's because you're the best dog ever."

Colt pressed a palm to Dani's forehead. "You should rest."

"I've been resting ever since I woke up."

"Colt's right, you shouldn't be walking."

"Colt can carry me."

He held up his hands. "Not a chance. Ben's liable to shoot me on sight."

Heather set down her stethoscope with a thunk. "I've got the next best thing. Wait here."

She disappeared out the door and Colt leaned toward Dani for a hug. "There was a while there where I thought I lost you."

"Sorry."

"I'm glad you're okay."

"Me, too." She fidgeted in the bed. "Last thing I remember, you were in a standoff with that Ben guy. I thought we were all going to die."

Colt swallowed.

"Heather said he's in charge."

"That's right."

Dani chewed on her lip. "We've been talking and she told me about the farm and what they're doing here and what her life was like before." She glanced at the bed. "She's nice."

"Seems that way." To see Dani open up to a stranger tugged at Colt's heart. The girl had been through so much, he wasn't sure she'd ever accept anyone except their ten-person family. He encouraged her to continue with a squeeze of her hand.

"All those things I said before, about burning the place down and not caring about the people here—"

Colt knew what she was going to say, but he waited until she found the courage.

"I was wrong. We should have tried to talk to them from the beginning."

Colt reached out and ruffed her hair and Dani batted him away. He wanted to tell her that he was beginning to agree and that maybe he shouldn't have been so quick to judge, but the door opened before he could.

"All right. It won't be the smoothest ride, but I've found a solution." Heather smiled at Colt. "If you can carry her outside, I can give you both a tour."

Ten minutes later, with blankets and pillows and Lottie balanced in Dani's lap, they were situated in a four-seat ATV. Heather cranked the engine and smiled at Colt from beneath a fur-trimmed hood. "So how much of the farm have you seen?"

He zipped up his jacket and thought it over. "The barns, the silos, the three fenced-in animal areas."

"So you haven't seen the orchards?"

Colt shook his head and they took off, bumping over snow and gravel and hard-packed earth until they crested the nearest hill. Trees in organized rows stretched down the other side.

"This is all yours?"

Heather nodded. "Apples, mostly. They do the best with harsh winters."

"Wow." Dani leaned forward from the back. "Think about all the things Anne could can. Apple pie filling, applesauce, apple butter, spiced apple rings, apple jelly."

Colt laughed. "Would you even eat half of those?"

"Beats canned peas."

Heather groaned. "I'll agree with you there. Those things smell nasty."

The ATV ambled down the hillside and Heather launched into a description of their farm in the summer months. They harvested everything from wheat to corn to beans and okra. An entire field was devoted to pumpkins and squash and in the fall they canned so many pickles they had to drive to Reno to scavenge for jars.

Colt was amazed. "How many people do you have?"

"Including the kids?" Heather counted up in her head. "Twenty-five. But the toddlers don't help much."

Size mattered. If they could accomplish all this with twenty-five, Colt wondered how much both farms could accomplish working together.

"Do you hunt?"

"Haven't had time. We've been getting by with the chickens and the pigs." Heather wrinkled her nose. "We eat a lot of eggs."

Hunting was something the Clifton farm excelled at. If they collaborated, the Clifton group could provide fresh game and the Jacobsons could provide extra harvest. It might be a match everyone found benefit from.

Colt ran a hand down his face as they turned back toward the main section of the farm. He'd underestimated the value of other people. Ben had protected his own, not acted like Jarvis. He should have given them some latitude.

Heather parked the ATV outside the medical building and Colt clambered down. He reached for Dani when a voice shouted out.

"Stop right there!"

Colt lifted his hands and turned around.

Ben Jacobson stood fifteen feet away in the snow, with a handgun aimed at Colt's chest.

Heather jumped out of the vehicle and ran around to the other side. She stood in front of Colt and blocked the shot. "Put it down, Ben. He's not the bad guy here."

"Get out of the way, Heather."

She palmed her hips. "No."

"I'm not going to ask again."

Heather shook her head. "What are you going to do, shoot me? You think that'll make Grandad proud? You shooting your only niece because you're too pigheaded to see what's right in front of you?"

With every word, Colt's admiration of Heather grew. He glanced at Dani. Her face had paled to match the snow. He whispered to her. "It'll be okay."

She shuddered and Lottie jumped off her lap and into the snow. Colt tried to catch her, but she wriggled free. "Lottie, no!" He shouted at her and twisted around, but Lottie was having none of it.

She trotted all seven pounds of herself right up to Ben's feet and began to bark. And bark, and bark, and bark.

He crouched down to her eye level. "Who are you?"

Colt could barely keep the emotion out of his voice. "That's Lottie, and if you so much as touch her, heaven help me, I'll kill you."

Ben stood up. "You'd kill me over a dog?"

"She saved my life." He glanced back at Dani. "And

she used to belong to someone who didn't survive in this new world." He swallowed. "So if you have any decency, you'll leave her alone."

Ben glanced at Heather and then back at Colt before lowering his weapon. "If Heather says you're all right, then I suppose you must be."

Dani patted the blanket. "Lottie, come here, girl."

The little dog took one sniff of Ben, barked again, and ran back to Dani in the ATV.

Ben huffed. "I don't think she likes me very much."

Heather rolled her eyes. "Can you blame her?"

CHAPTER TWENTY-NINE

TRACY

Clifton Compound
    Near Truckee, CA
    6:00 p.m.

The familiar canary-colored Jeep pulled up in the gravel drive and Tracy was the first one out the cabin door. Walter climbed down and Tracy ran to him, wrapping her arms around his middle as she pressed her face to his jacket.

He hugged her and the tightness lingering in her chest eased. "I told you it wouldn't be long."

She pulled back with a smile as Larkin hopped down from the other side and Ben Jacobson climbed out of the back seat. Tracy cocked her head. "What's going on?"

"I thought it was time the two families met." Walter glanced at Ben as he took in the sight of the compound. "We can help each other."

Tracy nodded as the three men from the Jacobson farm came down the steps to greet Ben. "I've been thinking the same thing."

A moment later, a pickup truck rolled in and a familiar bark rose above the rumbling engine.

"Lottie!" Tracy smiled as the little dog pawed at the back gate. Tracy scooped her up as Colt hoisted Dani from the back of the truck.

He carried her over to Tracy. "She's not supposed to walk for a while. Where should we go?"

Tracy pointed at the cooking cabin. "We're assembling in there." She reached out and squeezed Dani's arm. "I'm glad you're okay."

Colt carried Dani off and Tracy let Lottie down to follow them. Barry and Anne introduced themselves to Ben and ushered everyone inside. It was a tight squeeze, but they made it.

After coffees were distributed and everyone settled into a seat or a spot leaning against a wall, Walter spoke up. "I brought Mr. Jacobson here in hopes we could find a way to help each other. They have a working farm and so do we. If we pool our resources, we may be able to expand our operations and begin to rebuild what we've lost."

"You mean start a town?" Dani held her mug in both hands and blew across the surface. "Why would we want to do that?"

"Not a town, but a co-op."

Ben propped a hand on one knee. "We've got an

established orchard and have a decent wheat harvest in the fall. What do you all do here?"

Anne leaned in. "We're avid hunters and we process and preserve everything that comes in the door. If it can be canned or dehydrated, we do it."

Walter spoke up. "And now that we're on the farm, we're HAM radio operators."

Tracy glanced at her husband. If he was willing to share their radio secret, then he must truly believe in the possibility of the farms joining forces.

Ben perked up. "A radio? You mean there are people out there, talking to each other?"

Walter nodded. "It's sporadic, but yes. I broadcast relatively frequently, as do others. The chatter has dropped off a bit this winter, but it's still there. If we were in a city, I could broadcast on a radio station." He smiled at Barry. "It's a bit hard to manage that out here."

Tracy could almost see the gears turning in Ben's head. He hadn't thought about the broader picture and what it meant to communicate with people in other areas.

"How far does it go?"

"I've picked up people as far away as the Midwest."

"No way." Ben seemed impressed. He rubbed his chin. "With your hunting skills and the radio knowledge, I can see us working together. We could be the start of something new."

Colt chimed in. "Assuming we can keep from killing each other."

Ben snorted out a laugh. "True enough."

Colt held out his hand. "My apologies on trying to kill you."

Ben accepted with a shake. "Sorry Craig shot your daughter."

Tracy glanced at Colt. The man leaned back and looked at Dani, but he didn't correct Ben. Dani hid a smile. They were already father and daughter in all but name. It warmed her heart to see them both accept it.

She reached for her husband's hand. "If we survive this winter, I can see a whole new world opening up for us this year."

Anne, Barry, the rest of the room agreed.

Ben raised his mug. "Here's to the beginning of a new alliance."

Everyone took a sip and conversation broke out in pockets here and there. Brianna and Peyton talked to Craig in the corner. Ben and Colt thawed toward each other over reminiscing about the past. Larkin poked fun at Daniel's pickup truck.

It was like they had known each other for years.

Tracy reached over and took her daughter's hand and Madison smiled. Visions of her daughter growing up and getting married and starting a family rose in her mind. It wasn't the way she envisioned it even a year ago, but for the first time since the lights went out, she had real hope.

Maybe the future wouldn't be so grim after all.

* * *

Thank you for reading book eight in the *After the EMP* series!

Looking for more *After the EMP*? You can find the rest of the series on Amazon.

If you haven't read *Darkness Falls*, the exclusive companion short story to the series, you can get it for free by subscribing to my newsletter:

www.harleytate.com/subscribe

If you were hundreds of miles from home when the world ended, how would you protect your family?

Walter started his day like any other by boarding a commercial jet, ready to fly the first leg of his international journey. Halfway to Seattle, he witnesses

the unthinkable: the total loss of power as far as he
can see.

Hundreds of miles from home, he'll do whatever it takes
to get back to his wife and teenage daughter. Landing the
plane is only the beginning.

ACKNOWLEDGMENTS

Thank you for reading *Hope Stumbles*, book eight in the *After the EMP* saga.

It's been a long time since I've written about the Sloane family and I'm happy to be back with them again. With the introduction of new allies will come both challenges and a path forward. I'm excited to figure out where these new characters fit in the greater *After the EMP* story and I hope you'll come along for the ride!

As I've mentioned before, I do try to be as realistic as possible with everything I write. However, I do take occasional liberties, mostly with real names and places, but also occasionally with facts (like which animals tend to contract rabies in the Sierra Nevadas!), for the sake of the story. I hope you don't mind.

If you enjoyed this book and have a moment, please consider leaving a review on Amazon. Every one helps new readers discover my work and helps me keep writing the stories you want to read.

I had originally planned on moving back to my *Nuclear Survival* series after finishing this book, but now I'm reconsidering writing book nine of *After the EMP* first. After a few days to give it some thought, I'll be back in the trenches writing away. Look for a new book (of whichever series I decide to continue) soon.

Happy reading,

Harley

ABOUT HARLEY TATE

When the world as we know it falls apart, how far will you go to survive?

Harley Tate writes edge-of-your-seat post-apocalyptic fiction exploring what happens when ordinary people are faced with impossible choices.

Harley's first series, *After the EMP*, follows ordinary people attempting to survive in a world without power. When the nation's power grid is wrecked, it doesn't take long for society to fall apart. The end of life as we know it brings out the best and worst in all of us.

The apocalypse is only the beginning.

Contact Harley directly at:
www.harleytate.com
harley@harleytate.com

Made in the USA
Columbia, SC
08 January 2021